FALLING STAR

FALLING STAR

Robert Rayner

James Lorimer & Company Ltd., Publishers
Toronto

James Lorimer & Company Ltd. acknowledges the support of the Ontario Arts Council. We acknowledge the support of the Government of Canada through the Book Publishing Industry Development Program (BPIDP) for our publishing activities. We acknowledge the support of the Canada Council for the Arts for our publishing program. We acknowledge the support of the Government of Ontario through the Ontario Media Development Corporation's Ontario Book Initiative.

Library and Archives Canada Cataloguing in Publication
Rayner, Robert, 1946-
Falling star / Robert Rayner.

(Sports stories)
ISBN 978-1-55277-505-9

I. Title. II. Series: Sports stories (Toronto, Ont.)

PS8585.A974F34 2010   jC813'.6   C2010-900283-0

James Lorimer & Company Ltd.,
Publishers
317 Adelaide St. West
Suite 1002
Toronto, Ontario
M5V 1P9
www.lorimer.ca

Distributed in the United States by:
Orca Book Publishers
P.O. Box 468
Custer, WA USA
98240-0468

Printed and bound in Canada.
Manufactured by Friesens Corporation in Altona, Manitoba, Canada in February 2010. Job # 53490

CONTENTS

For Seth

ACKNOWLEDGEMENTS

Thanks to Caira Clark and her friends in Josh Cheney's Language Arts class at St. Stephen Middle School, New Brunswick, for the list of (acceptable) put downs and expletives.

1 CANTERBURY

The way you did it was this, you kicked the ball low on the side, kind of stroking it with your foot, so the spin you put on it made it bend at the same time that gravity made it dip. When you kicked it just right — at just the right angle, and with just the right power — it was a sure goal.

Edison Flood placed the ball and backed up a few paces. He trotted forward and blasted it. The goalkeeper dived hopelessly as the ball rocketed into the top corner of the net. It didn't really count for anything because Edison was taking practice shots in the pre-game warm-up, but his teammates on the Canterbury Middle School Eagles applauded, grinning. One said, "You make it look easy."

It was easy for him. He didn't know why. It was just something he'd always been good at. Some kids were good at math, and some at art, and some at computers. Edison was good at kicking and dribbling a soccer ball. He'd been labelled a soccer "wonder kid" at age eight, and had been to so many soccer academies, enrichment clinics, and elite camps he couldn't remember them all.

He didn't look like a super athlete. He was thin and pale, with fine blond hair that hung across his forehead in a thin, wispy fringe, and a narrow face that curved inwards under his cheekbones. He thought he looked more like one of those old poets in English class than a soccer player.

Edison never thought about how he managed to dribble the ball with such control, and shoot so accurately and fiercely. It was something he'd been doing since he was a toddler playing by himself, kicking a ball through the tufts of grass on the sand dunes around the lake near his home. He moved the ball into the shallows before booting it, so that it wouldn't go far and he wouldn't lose it. After piloting the ball around the patches of spiky grass in the soft sand, going past defenders was easy, and shooting without water slowing the ball felt like unleashing a missile.

There had been a time when his coaches wouldn't let him practice shooting before a game, keeping his skill a kind of secret weapon. But now every team he played against knew about him. It didn't matter. Goalkeepers still couldn't stop his shots, and he scored at least once in just about every game. He was top scorer in the Central Canada Elite League, and he went into every game confident of scoring, just as he was confident he'd score today.

Unless it happened again.

He pushed the memory away.

The Eagles were playing the Mississauga Marauders and they had to win to stay at the top of the league.

He had time to glance around as the teams lined up to shake hands before the kick off. The covered stands on one side of the field and the bleachers on the other were almost full. Several hundred supporters showed up for every Eagles game, not just students, but people from the town of Canterbury itself. His glance moved on to the school buildings — the low classroom units, the science block with all the labs, the physical arts block with the two gyms, the music block with the theatre. Beyond the school grounds, the subdivisions of Canterbury stretched towards the sprawl of Toronto.

As the referee whistled for the start, Edison, at centre forward, tapped the ball to his teammate beside him. Suddenly the memory of the previous game returned — the free kick a few metres outside the penalty area, perfect for bending and dipping the ball … the wall of players forming between him and the goal … the keeper crouching ready … his teammates watching … the crowd tense and silent … his easy, almost casual, trot towards the ball …

Then — the miss, the ball soaring high and wide of the goal.

It hadn't mattered because they were leading by two goals and it was near the end of the game. He'd laughed about it afterwards, while his teammates and the coach teased him. But the memory gnawed at him. He never missed, not like that. The ball must have been inflated to the wrong pressure. Or he'd taken his eye off it at the last second. Or it was wet and his cleat had slipped as it connected. It wouldn't happen again.

Would it?

★ ★ ★

Late in the game, with the Eagles and the Marauders tied at one goal each, Edison got the ball at the corner of the Mississauga goal area. He'd already scored — an easy tap into the net after the goalkeeper had failed to hold another forward's shot — and now he could score again to keep his team on top of the league. He could shoot for the far corner of the net, curving the ball around the goal-keeper, who was at the near post. An opposing defender was approaching, but there was plenty of time to get the shot away.

Suddenly the defender was on him, whisking the ball from his feet and clearing it.

He didn't understand what had happened. He remembered sizing up the shot, seeing the approaching defender, and preparing to shoot, all in a split second, then … nothing, until the defender robbed him of the ball. Had he blacked out? It was like a movie with part of a scene missing, so the action jumped and didn't make sense.

The game ended a few minutes later. The Eagles captain, with a sideways glance at Edison, said, "We should have won. We had a chance to score at the end."

Edison looked at the ground.

The coach looked curiously at him and asked, "Why didn't you shoot?"

"Didn't have time."

The coach raised his eyebrows.

Edison's mother, who came to watch all his games, greeted him with, "You played well."

She was wearing a black pantsuit, and her hair was a shiny blond helmet. Her lips were bright red and her eyebrows looked as if they'd been drawn on her face with a fine marker. She read the evening news on TV and was on her way to the studio.

The Eagles coach called, "Thank you for coming to watch, Mrs. Flood."

She smiled graciously. "It was a good game." She spoke in her "TV voice" all the time. Edison never knew whether to be proud of her or embarrassed.

"We'll miss Edison," the coach went on. "And we'll miss seeing you on the sideline."

It was Edison's last game for the Eagles. His mother had been transferred to the Maritimes, where the TV station had a new affiliate in Saint John. They were going to live in a little town called Brunswick Valley. He was going to start school there, then transfer to High Park Memorial Academy, a boarding school that specialized in sports. The Eagles coach had recommended Edison to High Park, but Edison would still need a trial to comply with school policy. The High Park soccer coach said his team and Brunswick Valley School had a game in October, and that could count as the trial if Edison played for Brunswick Valley.

Mrs. Flood shook hands with the Eagles coach. "Thank you for all you've done for Edison."

The coach shook Edison's hand and said, "Good luck."

As Edison and his mother walked away, she looked at Edison from the corner of her eye and asked, "Right at the end of the game — why didn't you shoot?"

He shrugged. "Dunno."

"Or pass," she went on. "You could easily have passed."

"I know."

"Are you sure you're all right?"

He mumbled, "Yeah."

But he wasn't. That strange nagging feeling was still there.

2 BRUNSWICK VALLEY

One minute Edison was lying in bed puzzling over why he'd failed to shoot against the Marauders, the next he was reliving the game. A dream … He's playing in his pajamas, so everyone is looking at him. He realizes that they aren't looking at him because he is wearing his pajamas, but because they expect him to do something. The problem is, he doesn't know what. He tries to shout, "What do you want me to do?" but he can't speak. The coach is calling and pointing. It's not just the Canterbury coach, but all the coaches he's had in the last few years, since he's been regarded as a future star. He doesn't know where on the field he's supposed to go. He blunders a few steps in one direction, but the coaches are still pointing and calling, so he tries a different tack. He doesn't know where the ball is, but he keeps running in case it appears. And it does — but now he can't move. He feels as if he has weights in his soccer shoes. He is still straining to move when he wakes up.

Edison lay for a moment, trying to remember when Canterbury's next game was, worrying that he would choke again. Then he remembered. There wouldn't be another Canterbury game. For a few seconds he felt better, until he thought of playing for High Park, where the expectations would be even greater. If he choked for High Park, it would be not just embarrassing, but would probably cost him his place on the team, even at the Academy. He turned his thoughts to Brunswick Valley School. His mother had told him to think of it as just a convenient stop-gap between playing for Canterbury and High Park. Surely he could mess up there without anyone noticing. His mother said the school had only about two hundred students, and that was from kindergarten to grade twelve. Perhaps it was so small it wouldn't have a soccer team. Perhaps they didn't even play soccer in Brunswick Valley. All they did in those little coastal towns in the east was eat fish and play fiddles, wasn't it? He could start a new sport, something he wouldn't have to worry about, something without even a ball — swimming, or the long jump, or crosscountry running — something where he could be a total klutz and it wouldn't matter!

★ ★ ★

Three days later, Edison was standing behind the two-storey brick building that was Brunswick Valley

School, watching a scrimmage going on at the other end of the Back Field. The kids had told him the field was called that because it was at the back of the school. He thought a better name for it would be the Back of Beyond Field, because of the scrubby woods growing close to the lines on every side except the one facing the school. It was his first practice with Brunswick Valley, and he'd expected to find the team awaiting directions from the coach, not actually playing. He didn't feel he had the right to barge in on their game.

The coach called to one of the boys, who plodded across the field, planted himself in front of Edison, and said, "Hey. I'm Toby."

Although Toby was only medium height, Edison felt dwarfed by the boy's broad, chunky build. Toby was panting, and his pale face was blotched with red from exertion. He ran his hand over his fair hair, which was styled in a neat brush cut.

Edison nodded. "Hi. I'm Edison."

Toby put his hands behind his back, then clasped them in front of him, and finally stuffed them in the pockets of his baggy shorts, which billowed around his thick legs. "I guess I'm supposed to welcome you to the team."

"Thanks."

"You're from Canterbury — right? Near Toronto?"

"Part of it, really."

"Wow. I expect you find Brunswick Valley a bit different."

Edison thought, *And how!* But he didn't say anything.

"Want to come and play?" asked Toby.

"Sure. Thanks."

"Watch where you walk." Toby pointed to a pile of pellets like earth-coloured birds' eggs.

"What is it?"

"Moose poop." He pointed to another smaller pile nearby. "And that's deer poop. It's not bad if you get it on your shoes. In fact it's quite clean, as far as poop goes." He chuckled. "I tell visiting teams, ones who don't know any better, it's bear poop. Gets them nervous before we start the game."

"But it's not bear poop?"

"Nah." Toby veered toward the woods bordering the field and pointed to a patty of what looked like chewed-over and spat-out blueberries. "*That's* bear poop."

As they walked on, Toby nodded toward the coach, who had a mess of black hair that hung to his shoulders. "That's Mr. Field. Good name for a soccer coach, eh? Mr. *Field*. His nickname's Ice. He says it's because it makes Ice Field — get it? — but really it's because when he was in high school, before he got old and became a teacher, all the kids thought he was cool as ice."

The players were now standing around their coach,

watching Edison approach. He knew he'd be doing the same if he was in their place. What was a new player doing arriving near the end of the season? How come he expected just to walk into an established team?

Mr. Field said, "I've asked Toby to introduce the new member of our team."

Toby jerked his thumb at Edison and said, "Edison."

There was a chorus of "Hi, Edison," from the players.

Edison mumbled, "Hey."

"Do you want to tell us anything about yourself?" the coach asked.

Edison shook his head.

Toby picked up a soccer ball and said, "Come on, Edison. It's boys against girls." He added, grinning, "The girls are pitiful, and it's no contest, but it's good for them to play against us and see how the game should be played."

A tall girl, with long golden hair framing a perfectly oval face, grabbed the ball from him and said, "You're asking for it, Toe Fungus." She turned to Edison. "Hi, Edison. I'm Julie. I hope you're more of a gentleman than Toby." Turning back to Toby, she dropped the ball to her feet, taunting, "Bet you can't get it off me."

Julie dribbled backward with Toby in pursuit. Every time he lunged for the ball, she skipped away, laughing.

The coach said, "Welcome to the team, Edison. Where do you play?"

"Forward, if that's all right," he answered.

Edison suddenly realized how long it had been since a soccer coach hadn't known all about his soccer skills. He felt somehow lighter than he had for a long time at the prospect of a game.

"You can be a strike partner for Steve," Mr. Field went on. "He's usually on his own up front and would like some help. Isn't that right, Steve?"

The coach looked across at a tall, rangy boy with hair the colour of river mud flopping over his eyes. Steve, looking warily at Edison, nodded slowly.

The player beside Edison offered his hand in a formal gesture. "I'm Shay." Although he was short-er than Edison, he was more sturdily built. He had a round, serious face and a mop of dark hair.

As they shook hands, Julie circled back toward the group of players, with Toby still trying to rob her of the ball.

Shay said, "Excuse me." As Julie continued back-ward, he kneeled in her path, tucking his head down so that she fell over him. Toby collected the loose ball and said, "There — easy."

A short, slight girl with glasses, who had been stand-ing at the edge of the group, bobbed her head at Edi-son and murmured quickly, "I'm Linh-Mai. Pleased to meet you." She ran to tackle Toby, who stabbed the ball away, calling, "Edison — here."

Edison ran for the ball. Hearing feet approach-ing from behind at a run, he put his foot on the ball and rolled it out of his pursuer's way, spinning around at the same time. A blond ponytail behind a freckled, laughing face flashed past. He looked up and found an identical freckled, laughing face and ponytail confronting him. His first challenger, recovering and closing in from one side, said, "Hi. I'm Jillian," as the other, also moving in, said, "I'm Jessica." As Jillian tackled him, he feinted to take the ball right, but stepped over it and pushed it left, before collecting it and weaving easily around Jessica.

Toby shouted, "Shoot!"

Instinctively, Edison obeyed. He was between the goal area and the halfway line, and knew without looking exactly where the net was. The ball soared on a trajectory that started high and wide of the net, and Julie called, "Missed!" Then she, and the others, applauded as, at the last moment, the ball dipped and swerved into the top corner of the net.

Edison saw Steve looking at him and suddenly felt as if he was showing off. He wished he hadn't taken the shot.

As the scrimmage resumed, Edison wondered when they would start the real practice. Then he realized how many skills they were practising by playing in the confined area laid out by Mr. Field. He ticked them off in his head: creating space, keeping possession, dribbling and passing under pressure, tackling, and intercepting.

Near the end of the practice, Mr. Field called

Edison to the sideline. "Do you know we won our division of the provincial league this season, and we had the most points out of all the teams in the five divisions?" Edison shook his head, trying not to look surprised, as the coach went on. "Now we go on the Champions Tour. Can you come?"

"What is it?"

"It's to make sure the team with the most points doesn't have them just because its division is weaker than the others. We have to keep our game point average while we play the winners of the other divisions. It means we have to win at least two games, and draw at least one."

"I don't want to take someone's place."

"You won't. Right now, we don't even have a substitute."

Edison rejoined the game as Steve robbed Linh-Mai of the ball by shoulder-charging her. He kicked it ahead and elbowed Jillian aside as she tried to intercept. Mr. Field called, "Steve, take it easy." Steve took a long shot at goal but missed. He caught Edison's eye and looked away quickly. But the glance was long enough for Edison to feel it like an accusation, as if Edison's shot had been a challenge that Steve had failed to meet. Edison wanted to say something, but knew nothing helped when you missed a shot.

After the practice, Mr. Field told the team, "We leave the school at eleven o' clock on Saturday morning with Foote Transport. That's eleven o' clock, Toby, not eleven-fifteen or eleven-thirty. Remember, we'll be on the road for four days, so make sure you have all your overnight stuff as well as your soccer kit."

As Edison walked to the change rooms, he glanced at the information Mr. Field had given him about the Champions Tour. The fourth school Brunswick Valley played was High Park. He felt the feeling of anxiety return, clouding the enjoyment he'd got from the scrimmage.

3 THE VAN

On Saturday morning, Mrs. Flood stopped the car in the road beside the school gate and said, "What a *gorgeous* little bus."

She pointed to the van that was parked in front of the school. It was bright yellow, with huge, pastel-coloured flowers painted on the sides and roof. As they looked, the door opened and the driver climbed out. He was tall and broad, and wore a grey, oil-smeared muscle shirt. His baggy camouflage pants came down to the top of his ankles, leaving his black work boots exposed. His head was shaved, except for a strip of spiked red hair down the middle.

Mrs. Flood caught Edison's eye and grinned. "What would the parents in Canterbury do if the team bus driver looked like that?"

Edison grinned back. "They'd probably have him arrested."

Mr. Field, in torn jeans and a long black coat, his hair as wild as it had been the previous day, ran down the steps from the school door and greeted the driver. "Hey, Grease."

They high-fived, Mr. Field staggering back slightly as the driver's hand slammed into his.

"Who's the wild man?" asked Mrs. Flood.

"That's our coach."

"I'm surprised the principal allows him to dress like that, even if it is Saturday."

"He dresses like that at school."

A battered half-ton truck, belching smoke, swung into the school driveway. Toby was squeezed into the cab with a woman who had the same chunky build and fair hair as his own. She struggled from the cab, grabbed Toby in a hug, and said, "Behave yourself or there'll be no French fries for a month."

"Who's that?" asked Mrs. Flood.

"He's called Toby and he plays fullback."

Toby was wearing baggy cargo pants, and his un-tucked shirt hung below his parka. Edison was dressed the way the Eagles coach always demanded, in a dress shirt and tie. He was afraid he looked preppy.

"And who are they?" A flatbed truck stopped in the road to let Shay, Julie, and Linh-Mai cross.

"That's Shay, the captain," said Edison. He was pleased to see Shay was wearing a dress shirt, although he had no tie, and that the girls — Julie in cord pants and a wool jacket, Linh-Mai in a mauve skirt and short white coat — seemed to have taken at least a little care to dress smartly.

"What about the princess and the pixie?" his mother asked.

"The tall one's Julie — she plays midfield. The other one's Linh-Mai, who plays fullback with Toby."

The girls, who were holding hands, squealed as the truck driver blasted his horn and grinned down at them. He called to Shay, "What have you got that I haven't?" Then, as he pulled away, "Good luck, you guys. Give 'em heck."

Julie waved and shouted, "Thanks, Uncle Charlie."

"Do you suppose everybody in town knows everybody else — and what they're doing?" asked Mrs. Flood. Suddenly serious, she added, "I hope this works out for you — coming to a new school and playing with a new team, all because of my job."

"I don't mind."

"I talked it over with your father and he thought it would be a good move."

Mr. Flood was vice president of a mining company and was working on a project in South America for a year. He called at least once a week and always asked Edison how he was doing in school and at soccer. Edison liked telling him about the games, but he hadn't mentioned the times he'd choked.

Mrs. Flood went on, "I hope this team is good enough for you. But even if it's not, it will be good experience until you start at High Park."

Shay had found a soccer ball, which he and Toby were passing back and forth in the school driveway while Julie and Linh-Mai tried to intercept. Shay lobbed the ball high over the girls. Toby headed it and it sailed over the school fence, where it bounced from the sidewalk onto the roof of the Floods' car, before rolling into the road. Toby ran out to retrieve it. As he passed the car he looked in and said, "Sorry." He looked again and added, "Oh — hi, Edison."

Edison jumped out and said quickly, "See you, Mom," hoping his mother would stay in the car.

Mrs. Flood climbed out. "I'll see you off."

Mr. Field strode to greet her, holding out his hand.

She said, "How do you do. I'm Edison's mother."

Mr. Field said, "Hey, Mrs. Flood." His voice was gravelly and hoarse.

She turned to the driver. "And this is …?"

The driver had been leaning against the van. He straightened and offered his hand to Mrs. Flood, who took it after a moment's hesitation. He was nearly two heads higher than she stood in high heels, and her hand disappeared completely in his.

"Mr. Foote," said Mr. Field.

"How do you do, Mr. Foote?"

Mr. Foote said, "Grease."

"Sorry?"

Mr. Foote looked at Mr. Field, who said, "He means you can call him Grease. That's what everyone calls him, except the kids. He's Mr. Grease to them."

"I absolutely *love* your darling van," said Edison's mother.

Mr. Grease grunted.

Linh-Mai was struggling to open the door. Mr. Grease opened it for her and picked up her two bags. He held out his hand to help her climb inside, and passed the bags to her. He did the same for Julie. Shay and Toby climbed in.

Edison said again, "See you, Mom."

Before he could move out of reach, his mother leaned forward, hugged him, and whispered, "The coach of your soccer team is Mr. *Field*, and the driver of the soccer team is Mr. *Foote*. That's *so* cute. It's like something out of a kids' story. I'd picture them as little furry creatures if I hadn't seen them in real life." She kissed him on the cheek, and said louder, "Play well. Make me proud."

He felt himself blushing as he climbed in.

The four rows of seats were covered in leopard-print fabric, which also covered the sides and roof of the van. A pair of fuzzy dice hung from the rearview mirror. Julie and Shay were sitting on the front bench seat, while Toby was stretched out at the back.

Julie, giggling, mimicked, "Make me proud," as Edison passed her.

He paused to grumble, "How come I'm the only one whose mother sees him off?"

The Van

"I tell Ma she can't come," said Julie. "If she did, she'd be like a total embarrassment, crying and stuff."

"She'd cry — because you're going away for a few days?"

"Cause she wouldn't have a babysitter for my little sis for a few days."

Edison slid into the seat behind her and Shay, and found himself beside Linh-Mai, who was so small she'd been hidden by the seat in front. She was the youngest on the team — he'd heard Toby teasing her about it — and she looked it, she was so small and slight. Her glasses were tinted dusky red and had delicate gold arms. Even with the tinted lenses, he could see how dark her eyes were. Tiny red-streaked braids hung at the front of her black shoulder-length hair.

He wondered whether she wanted the seat all to herself but, before he could speak, she offered, "You can sit by the window if you like."

He muttered, "Thanks."

As she put her legs on the seat for him to climb past, she said, "Your ma looks like a model."

"She reads the news on television. That's why she's dressed up. She's on her way to the studio now. She's going to be on Channel Five."

"Cool."

Edison said, "Yeah — cool."

His mother waved as they pulled out of the school gate.

4 ON THE ROAD

Edison sat with his nose against the van window, looking at the curious mixture of houses that made up Brunswick Valley. Some were tidy and modern, like the houses in Canterbury. Some were old and elegant, like the houses around the lake where he'd grown up. A lot looked as if they might collapse at any moment.

On Main Street, which had a convenience store at one end and a dollar store at the other and not much in between, the van stopped in front of a large house set back from the road. The twins raced down the driveway, ponytails swinging behind them, and sat behind Edison.

Mr. Grease turned off Main Street and stopped where a thin, wiry girl with a rosy sunburned complexion waited on the sidewalk. Edison remembered this was Amy, the goalkeeper. She had wavy brown hair that hung halfway down her back, and the sun glinted on her braces when she smiled as the van pulled up. She started talking as soon as Mr. Field opened the door for her, and continued as she climbed in. "Wow, I love this van. The outside with all the flowers is so keen — hi, Shay, hi, Julie — but the inside is even better with this furry stuff all over — hi, Linh-Mai, hi, Edison — and this is just so exciting — hi, Jillian, hi, Jessica — because I've never been on a trip like this. Well, of course, I've been on lots of trips — hi, Toby — like to museums and art galleries and concerts and stuff, but not a *soccer* trip ..."

She sat beside Toby, who said, "Do you come with earplugs?"

She nudged him. "Oh — you."

The next stop was for Matthew, Jason, and Brandon. Matthew was sitting on the curb with his feet in the gutter, absorbed in a book of math puzzles. Behind him, Jason and Brandon kicked a rock around on the sidewalk. Matthew sat with the twins, while Jason and Brandon squeezed into the rear seat beside Toby and Amy.

Steve waited by the road a little further on, in front of what Edison first thought was a shed. Seeing two little windows on each side of the door, Edison realized it was Steve's house. It leaned to one side, and black tarpaper showed at one corner of the roof where the shingles were missing. Around it, on beaten-down dirt, were two rusted jeeps without wheels, a woodpile covered by an orange tarp, and a shiny red ATV. A thin coil of grey smoke drifted from a metal stovepipe that stuck out from one side of the house.

Linh-Mai whispered, "Steve lives with just his mom. Don't ask him about his dad. He's inside."

"Inside?"

"In jail. For drugs and stuff."

Steve was wearing grey sweatpants and a black sweater with the sleeves pushed up. As he climbed in, one of the sleeves slipped down, revealing a hole in the elbow. Steve pushed it back.

Mr. Field asked, "No jacket, Steve?"

"It's not cold."

"I've got a spare any time you want one."

"Yeah. Thanks."

He sprawled on the other side of Linh-Mai.

"That's everybody," said Mr. Field, looking around from the front passenger seat. "Let's hit the highway, Grease."

They drove out of town and headed north, passing a sign stating *Centreville 200 kms*. Their first game was against Centreville Middle School.

Mr. Field commented, "We'll be there by two o' clock, in good time for the kickoff at three."

Matthew's voice came from behind Edison. "If we continue to travel at our present average speed of sixty-five kilometres per hour over a distance of two hundred kilometres we will arrive at fourteen forty-three."

From the back Toby called, "Thanks, Einstein."

Linh-Mai confided, "It freaks me out when Matthew does stuff like that in his head."

Steve asked suddenly, "How many goals did you get this season?"

"Me?" Edison said.

"Yeah."

"A few."

"How many?" Steve pressed.

"Twenty-five."

Steve swore quietly. "You may as well have my place on the team now."

Linh-Mai said, "Don't be silly. You're always complaining about being our only goal scorer. It'll be great having two strikers."

"Who needs two when you've got a superstar from Toronto?" said Steve. He was silent for a few seconds, then muttered, "I know who'll be sitting on the bench this trip."

In front of Edison, Julie was describing a soccer move to Shay. She broke off and leaned forward to study his face. He was asleep. She made herself comfortable by leaning against him. On the other side of Linh-Mai, Steve opened a soccer magazine. On the back seat, Toby sprawled with his eyes closed as Amy prattled, "Mum and me saw this great movie last night. It was about this girl who wanted to play soccer for her school but ..." She stopped and nudged Toby. "Are you listening?"

Toby started and opened his eyes. "'Course I am."

Amy looked carefully at him before continuing. "... But only boys were allowed on the team so she dressed up as a boy and ..."

Toby's eyes slowly closed.

In front of them, Matthew was poring over his book of math puzzles, while the twins giggled over a soccer joke book.

Jillian called out, "Did you hear about the goalkeeper who let in five goals in the first ten minutes of a game? He was so upset he put his head in his hands ... and dropped it."

Everyone laughed except Edison. He felt for the goalkeeper. Letting in five goals was as bad as missing five goals. The keeper must have choked.

5 CENTREVILLE

Centreville seemed to be made up of one subdivision after another. In between were strip malls offering the same stores and services — hairdressers, convenience stores, takeouts, Sears outlets, liquor stores. It was like being back in Canterbury, except it was smaller.

As Edison gazed out the window, he became aware of Linh-Mai craning her head to see past him.

She murmured, "I wonder what the Centreville kids are like? Do you suppose they take soccer seriously, like getting good grades at school?"

There was a tremor in her voice. Edison had been trained to prey on players who revealed weakness like that. They were easily intimidated — by a fierce shot aimed right at them, or a dribbling trick that left them looking stupid, or a crunching tackle. He could always get past them — at least, he could before the choking started. Now he wasn't so sure.

Linh-Mai had taken off her glasses and was chewing on one of the arms. Suddenly he felt sorry for her, for her timidity and anxiety. He hoped there was no one on the Centreville team who would set out to humiliate her the way he would if he was playing against her.

The talk in the van died away as Mr. Grease drove through the town. When he stopped for a traffic light, with Centreville Middle School visible at the end of the street ahead, Mr. Field turned and asked, "Why so quiet?"

Shay glanced around at his teammates. "We're nervous."

Mr. Field nodded. "Nerves are good. They get the adrenalin flowing."

Edison thought, *How many times have I heard that?* He knew it was true, but that didn't stop the churning stomach, and the dry throat, and the cold sweat that were already assailing him, and that he knew would only get worse the closer he got to kickoff.

Mr. Grease parked the van in front of the school and Mr. Field led the team to the playing field beside it. Houses stretched away in every direction, and the school, two storeys, with white aluminum siding and lots of windows, looked like just another big suburban home. Although it was Saturday afternoon, students filled the bleachers.

As Edison and his teammates trotted on to the field, Amy started, "I like Centreville's yellow shirts but their shorts are a bit *too* green. If I played for them I'd ask the coach if we could have more of an *olive* green ..." She took her place in one of the goals, where she continued talking while Shay and Steve took shots at her. Edison had expected Mr. Field to direct some kind of warm-up, like his former coaches had always done, but he and Mr. Grease had the hood of the van open and were peering at the engine. Linh-Mai, Julie, and the twins were playing dodge ball. Toby joined in and Julie hit him with her first shot. When she complained, "You're too easy," he replied, "I need a rest, anyway," and lay down in the middle of the pitch.

Edison decided to go through his Eagles pre-game routine. He jogged slowly across the pitch. He returned, jogging backwards. He sprinted across, collected a soccer ball he found on the other side of the field, and sprinted back, keeping it close to his feet. With his old team, all the players had done this in a line, and he felt strange doing it by himself. The Eagles had always finished their routine standing in a circle with their arms around one another's shoulders and their eyes closed, while the coach talked softly about the goals they were going to score, and the tackles they were going to make, and the defeat they were going to inflict on their opponents. The coach had called it envisaging and focusing. He'd ended every warm-up by repeating the words "focus" and "envisage" over and over while the players stood in their huddle. By the time the coach finished, Edison had always been convinced he was going to play well and score — until those last few games.

He stood with his head down and his eyes fixed on the grass, envisaging the game with Centreville so he didn't see Linh-Mai and Toby cautiously approach. He started when Linh-Mai said, "Are you all right?" and Toby asked, "Are you saying your prayers?"

"I'm envisaging and focusing."

"You're what?"

"Thinking about the game," said Edison. "We used to do it at my old school."

"Did it do any good?" asked Toby.

"It seemed to help."

"Can we do it?" said Linh-Mai.

"What do we have to do?" asked Toby.

"You stand in a circle and close your eyes, and you think about tackling and scoring and winning and stuff."

They stood in a circle with their arms around one another's shoulders and their eyes closed.

After a few seconds Toby said, "What do you think we'll have for supper?"

Linh-Mai said, "Focus!"

Shay and Julie wandered across.

"Are you having a séance?" Julie asked.

"We're focusing," said Toby.

"And envisaging," Linh-Mai added.

"Wanna try it?" said Toby.

Shay and Julie joined the circle.

The referee arrived on the pitch and the teams gathered around their coaches.

Mr. Field said, "Centreville doesn't get many goals, but doesn't let in many, either. We have to stop them scoring, because if they do score, they'll pack their defence and it'll be tough breaking them down. So we'll concentrate on defence, and go with only one striker. That'll be you, Steve, in the first half. You can run yourself into the ground trying to score, because Edison will take over from you after the break and do the same thing. Apart from that ..." he waved his hand in the direction of the field. "... just go play. Do your best — but don't forget it's just a game."

Edison remembered other coaches saying that. The difference with Mr. Field was that he really seemed to mean it.

The teams lined up to shake hands, Brunswick Valley in all blue, Centreville in green and yellow. Edison was beside Linh-Mai in the line. She'd tied a red strap around her head to hold her glasses in place. As she shook hands with a small red-haired girl with freckles, she confided to her in a shaky voice, "I'm some nervous."

The girl smiled and said, "Me, too."

Edison thought, *Loser talk*. His coaches had always told him you couldn't afford loser talk.

But what was worse? Loser talk, or being afraid of screwing up?

Edison took his place on the bench and surveyed the Centreville lineup. Like Brunswick Valley, they seemed to be playing with only one striker, a tall gawky boy with thin legs and bony knees. Edison guessed heading the ball would be his specialty. The centre half, whose name was Lily — he'd heard her teammates calling her — was tall too, but rugged.

He turned his attention to his own team. Shay stood calmly at midfield. Julie, beside him, jogged on the spot as if she couldn't wait for the game to start. Behind them, Toby leaned against one of Amy's goalposts, occasionally nodding as she talked, while Linh-Mai stood nearby chewing her fingernails. Edison wanted to run across and tell her she had to relax in order to play well. In the centre of the field, Steve stood with one foot on the ball and his arms folded. Edison could see the arrogant confidence of a striker in the way he coolly surveyed his opponents, and in his relaxed stance. Edison wished he could get back that confidence.

The referee whistled for the kickoff. Steve tapped the ball to Jillian and raced toward the Centreville goal. Jillian returned the ball, which Steve collected just in front of Lily. She moved to tackle him but he turned and backed into her, keeping the ball close to his feet. She loomed over him, her arms almost around him and her knees bumping against the backs of his legs, un-balancing him. Edison saw Steve's eyes roving, looking for support. The twins were on the wings, too far away to pass to. Brandon was running to help, but the tall centre forward, towering above him, was hard on his heels. Suddenly Steve was flat on his back and the ball spun away toward Brandon, who managed to poke it on to Jessica before the centre forward crashed into him, tumbling him to the ground. Jessica took the ball past one defender and centred it, but no one was there to take advantage of the cross. The Centreville goalkeeper caught the ball and rolled it out to Lily, who sent it over Shay and Julie for the home striker to receive on his head. The striker kept the ball in the air by repeatedly heading it, all the time moving toward the Brunswick Valley goal. It was some trick. As he neared the goal, with Toby moving cautiously to bar his way, and Steve racing at him from behind, he headed a weak shot, which Amy caught easily.

Edison wondered whether his teammates realized how dangerous the tall striker's heading skill made him. If he kept control of the ball as he headed it and moved toward the goal, there wasn't much Linh-Mai and Toby, his markers, could do about it. They couldn't tackle, because the ball was on his head, not at his feet. All they could do was stand in his way, but then they'd risk committing a foul, which could mean he would get a penalty kick. On the other hand, if they didn't bar his way, the centre forward had a clear path to goal.

As the first half wore on, Edison began to understand how Centreville had enjoyed such a successful
season. Mr. Field's assessment had been right. Their attack wasn't much, consisting of lobbing the ball to the
tall striker whenever he got near Amy's goal, but their
defence was solid. If Brunswick Valley advanced beyond
the halfway line, at least two home defenders immediately surrounded whoever had the ball, stifling movement and making it almost impossible to pass. On the
rare occasions when Steve managed to get away from
Lily and find some space, there was the lanky striker,
helping his defence and hanging over him like an over-
friendly giraffe.

Edison realized it wasn't just Centreville's suffo-
cating defence that was stifling every Brunswick Valley attack. It was more like his teammates were stifling
themselves. He thought of how they'd played in the
girls-against-boys scrimmage back at the school. Although that was fooling around rather than proper
soccer, they'd run with the ball, had created space for
themselves with constant movement, and had har-
ried whoever had the ball. Now the only player who
seemed to be doing that was Steve, who raced from
one end of the pitch to the other, helping his defence one minute, attacking the Centreville goal the
next. His method of attack was simple. He kicked the
ball ahead and ran after it, relying on speed to get to it
ahead of his opponents, or strength to hustle them off

it if they got there first.

Late in the first half, Steve passed to Shay from near his own goal. Shay kept possession while Steve ran past him into an attacking position. With two Centreville defenders closing in, Shay passed between them to Steve, who found himself with only Lily between himself and the goalkeeper. He moved right, then left, then right again, as he approached her. Lily moved with him, but stumbled at the third change of direction.

Edison thought, *She's tiring.*

Steve prodded the ball farther to the right to take it wide of Lily, but she stumbled into his path, knocking him over. By the time the referee awarded a free kick, the Centreville players were standing in a line between Steve and the goal, and the ball bounced harmlessly off them.

At halftime Steve pleaded with Mr. Field, "Let me stay on. Lily's getting tired and I can get past her now."

"You've done a great job wearing her down, but you're tiring too," said Mr. Field. "We'll stick with our plan of putting Edison on for the second half."

Steve flung himself on the bench, grumbling, "I would have scored."

When the teams lined up for the second half, Lily fixed her eyes on Edison. He tried to stare back, but she outlasted him and he looked away. Her thick legs and broad shoulders suggested he would come off second-best if they went for the ball at the same time, but he thought he had the speed to get past her. He read her expression as she stared — the pouty curl of her lip, the narrowed eyes — understanding it was meant to intimidate him. Normally it wouldn't have bothered him, because being good didn't just make him a star. It made him a target, as well. But with his nerves already on edge with the worry that he would choke again, he could feel Lily's taunting stare unsettling him more and more.

His first clash with her came ten minutes later when Brunswick Valley broke out of defence for the first time since the break. Edison was in midfield when Linh-Mai passed to him. As he trapped the ball, Lily rushed at him. He rolled it back onto his foot and flipped it over her head before running past her, skipping over her wildly flailing leg. Before he could collect the ball and continue upfield, she turned and tripped him. Under the guise of helping him up, she pinched his arm, muttering, "Think you're smart, don't you?"

Shay took a throw-in to Edison, who knew Lily was close behind. Edison trapped Shay's throw and backed into Lily, shielding the ball as she poked her shoe at it. He waited until her foot was stretching for the ball again, then rolled it backward through her legs, spinning around her at the same time. He collected the ball behind her as two more defenders closed in on him. Without looking up, he fired the ball over them at the Centreville goal. It was a long shot — so far out that no one would expect him to shoot from there, let alone score — but Edison knew those shots unsettled the goalkeeper and defence, making them nervous whenever he had the ball. And nervous defenders made mistakes. The keeper watched without moving as the ball seemed as if it would fly high across the goalmouth until, at the last second, it curled toward the net and hit the post.

Edison was feeling more confident by the minute. The choking incidents had surely been just a phase, and were in the past now.

But a few minutes later the anxiety was back.

Toby cleared the ball and Edison, running out of defence, reached it just before one of the Centreville backs. He looked for someone to pass to, but with his teammates still not running and chasing the way he'd seen them at practice, he found himself without support. He passed two defenders before looking up. Only Lily was in his way. If he got past her, it would be an easy goal, with only the keeper to beat. He could dribble past Lily, or simply use his speed and take the ball around her, or ...

He hesitated for only a fraction of a second, but she was on him with surprising speed. Her shoulder crashed into his chest, knocking him over as she took the ball and passed to one of her midfielders to start another Centreville attack.

As Edison picked himself up, he caught a glimpse

of Steve on the bench, shaking his head scornfully. He didn't blame Steve. Edison knew he should have scored.

Another ten minutes passed before Brunswick Valley managed to attack again. This time Julie scrambled the ball out of the goal area to Shay, who kept possession while Edison ran upfield. Shay looped the ball high over the two defenders who were marking Edison. As they watched the ball, Edison slipped away from them. He gauged where the ball would fall and caught it on his foot. Something — someone — loomed beside him. From the corner of his eye he saw it was Lily. Without thinking he flipped the ball over her, at the same time jumping clear of her lunge at him. She stumbled past him and fell, leaving Edison with an open goal except for the keeper, who slipped and fell as he raced forward to cut down Edison's shooting angle.

From the bench, Steve shouted, "Chip it over him!"

The goalkeeper scrambled to his feet and backpedalled frantically toward the net.

Steve shouted again, "Chip it over him!"

Edison considered chipping the ball. If he didn't kick it hard enough, it would land in the goalkeeper's arms, making Edison look foolish. On the other hand, if he kicked it too hard, it would sail over the crossbar, making Edison look like a complete idiot for missing an open goal.

Steve screamed, "Kick the freakin' ball!"

Something slammed into Edison's back and he

crashed to the ground on his face. Lily stepped over him and poked the ball back to the goalkeeper, who sent it high into Brunswick Valley's end of the pitch.

Centreville's goal, when it came late in the game, caught Edison by surprise. It caught his teammates, and even Centreville, by surprise too. Only a few minutes were left to play, and it seemed the game was at a goal-less stalemate. The defences had prevailed throughout, and neither side had come close to scoring, apart from Edison's two missed chances.

He watched as a mighty kick by Lily sent the ball from the Centreville goal area toward the Brunswick Valley end, high over the heads of all the defenders except Toby and Linh-Mai. The Centreville striker met the ball with his forehead, sending it back into the air over Toby and Linh-Mai. The striker ran between them and headed the ball on again. Amy rushed from her goalmouth and jumped for it, but couldn't reach it before he headed it one more time — over her outstretched arms and into the net.

The referee whistled for the end of the game.

Mr. Field greeted his team with, "Hard luck," and, "Well played" as they left the field. He said quietly to Edison, "You played a good game. Don't get uptight about pulling out of that shot. Things like that happen."

Edison mumbled, "Thanks," at the same time thinking, *But things like that don't happen to me. Or they never used to. And don't get uptight about it? Right — like Mr.*

Field knew what it was like to screw up in front of crowds of people.

Edison and his teammates boarded the van in gloomy silence.

6 THE DORCHESTER ALL STARS

They were still silent as Mr. Grease drove out of Centreville, heading north.

Suddenly Julie burst out, "We were pathetic."

"We were just unlucky," Shay protested.

"Like heck, we were unlucky," said Steve. He looked across Linh-Mai at Edison. "You should have scored at least once."

Edison had been gazing out the window at a bleak landscape of clearcut forest. He started. "Me?"

"Of course, you."

Linh-Mai, tense and wide-eyed, looked from Steve to Edison.

"That's not fair," said Shay. "Edison played a good game. He got round Lily lots of times …"

"Only because I wore her down in the first half."

"… And he did that great long shot that hit the bar."

"And he missed an open goal." Steve glared at Edison. "All you had to do was kick the ball over the keeper."

49

"Anyone can miss an open goal," Linh-Mai broke in. "Everything always happens so fast."

Steve snorted. "I would have scored."

Edison was sure Steve would have scored, as surely as he himself would have scored a few weeks ago, before the choking started. It was nice of Linh-Mai to say anyone could miss an open goal, but it had never happened to him before, and he knew if it continued he was finished as a striker.

He couldn't think of anything to say, except, "Sorry."

"That *really* helps," Steve scoffed.

Edison knew that if he was in Steve's place, he'd be upset too. If he was the team's best goal scorer, and he was left on the bench because there was a new striker, and he could only watch as his replacement lost the game … Yes, he'd be upset. But he found himself muttering, "Give it a rest."

Steve's voice rose. "Who are you telling to give it a rest?"

Julie turned around in her seat. "Leave it, Steve — all right?"

Shay added, "We didn't lose because of Edison, Steve. You know that."

Jillian called from the back, "We lost because we sucked — all of us."

"We sucked big time," Jessica put in.

Julie slumped back in her seat. "We're useless."

Mr. Field turned around from the front and ordered, "That's enough!" He told Mr. Grease, "Let's find somewhere to pull off the highway."

Mr. Grease turned sharply into a woods road and stopped.

Mr. Field said, "Everybody out."

Steve jumped out and stood with his arms folded and his back to everyone. Matthew, Jason, and Brandon walked slowly to the side of the dirt road with their heads down, their shoulders slumped, and their hands pushed deep into their pockets. Toby, Amy, and the twins stood in a silent huddle. Linh-Mai, Shay, and Julie joined them, and Julie muttered, "We may as well give up and go home now."

Edison wandered up the road and stood by himself.

Linh-Mai followed. "Don't mind Steve. He gets mad easily. He always goes on a rant when we lose. It's just the way he is."

"But he's right."

Toby, joining them, asked, "Right about what?"

"He's right that I should have scored. I lost the game for you. Sorry."

Toby punched him lightly on the shoulder. "If I said sorry every time I screwed up, I'd never stop talking."

He ambled back toward the van as Mr. Field called, "Someone get a ball. We're playing soccer — girls and Mr. Grease and me against the boys."

"I don't feel like playing," said Julie.

"Me neither," said Steve.

Mr. Field ignored them. He was already pacing out a length on the woods road and improvising goals with fallen branches. He started kicking the ball around with Mr. Grease. Amy, the twins, and Toby joined in. Amy miskicked the ball and it rolled toward Linh-Mai and Edison. Linh-Mai dribbled it back to the group.

"I guess you're on your own, Toby," said Mr. Field. "You're the only boy playing, so it's Julie, Linh-Mai, Jillian, Jessica, Amy, Mr. Grease, and me against you."

"You don't stand a chance," said Toby.

Julie, Amy, and Linh-Mai stood on one side of him, and the twins on the other, passing the ball backward and forward while he tried to intercept. When Linh-Mai charged past Toby and headed for the boys' goal, Matthew, Brandon, and Jason ran to stop her. She passed to Jessica, but Shay ran from the side of the road and took the ball. Julie, following hard on his heels, pushed him into the muddy ditch beside the road. While Matthew and Brandon pulled him out, the girls waltzed the ball easily past Toby and into the goal.

They danced in a circle, their hands in the air, chanting, "Girls rule!"

The boys ran back onto the pitch. Shay robbed Julie of the ball and the boys dribbled it toward the girls' end, where Mr. Field and Mr. Grease stood in the goal, filling it. Toby got the ball and, with a shout of "Edison!" chipped it over them. Edison ran forward and returned it to Toby, who rushed at the goal, but tripped and fell in a muddy puddle. When he stood, Amy burst out laughing and pointed at the dripping wet seat of his pants. Steve was still standing with his arms folded and his back to the game, until the girls scored again, and Shay pleaded, "Help us, Steve." He rushed onto the pitch and scored quickly. With the game tied, Mr. Grease picked up Linh-Mai and, while she held the ball between her feet, carried her above his head through the boys' goal. Mr. Field awarded victory to the girls, who repeated their dance, while Toby chanted, "No fair!" He stood in front of the boys, waving his arms like a music director as they joined in: "No fair!"

Mr. Field said quietly, "That's better."

As Mr. Grease swung the van back on to the highway, the twins started singing a country song, *Rollin' up the highway, baby, comin' home to you.* The rest of the girls joined in. When they came to the words, "Just can't wait …" Toby called, "Stop!" and sang the next two lines in a deep voice: "Just can't wait to see my dreamboat man tonight. My hunky man is waiting and he'll make me feel so-o-o right." He performed them with his arms crossed on his chest and his hands on his shoulders, pretending someone was hugging him, at the same time wiggling his shoulders with the beat. The girls, spluttering with laughter, resumed the song. The next time they came to Toby's lines, all the boys sang them with him. As he sang, Toby leaned toward Amy, rolling his eyes.

She screamed with laughter and said, "Stop or I'll wet myself."

Edison, his forehead resting on the window, couldn't help comparing this new team with his old one. If the Eagles had just lost an important game and couldn't afford to lose again, and had still to face High Park, the coach would have ranted at them, and analyzed everything they'd done wrong, warning them to make sure they played better — and won — next time. But all Mr. Field did was organize a crazy makeshift game of soccer on a muddy woods road in the middle of nowhere, and now the players were singing as if everything on the tour was going perfectly. He smiled at the contrast.

The third time the girls reached the boys' lines, Linh-Mai poked him in the ribs and said, "Wake up, Edison. Sing it," and he joined in.

He was surprised when the van passed a sign stating *Shanklin Bay*. He'd hardly noticed the scenery change from woods to suburbs. He peered around as they stopped in front of a row of cabins with an office in the middle. A flashing neon sign above it said, *Bay Line Motel. No Vacancy*.

"We have reservations," said Mr. Field.

Edison watched Mr. Field walk through the open door of the office. He saw the receptionist, a thin man in a shiny blue suit, consult his computer and shake his head. When Mr. Field produced a sheet of paper, the receptionist shrugged.

Mr. Field returned to the van. "The receptionist claims he has no record of our reservations."

"What are we going to do?" asked Shay.

Mr. Field grinned. "Follow me."

Edison thought of the tours he'd made with elite teams, staying in comfortable downtown hotels where the players were waved through reception. He smiled to himself again. You never knew what was going to happen next with Brunswick Valley.

The team climbed from the van. Edison was last. At the door of the office, Steve stood with his back to Edison, barring his way.

Inside, the receptionist was surveying the students, a worried look on his face.

Mr. Field said, "We'll wait in case you have a cancellation." He turned to the team. "Find something to do while you wait."

The twins started singing *Rock Me, Baby, All Night Long*. Julie and Shay joined in. Toby challenged Matthew to recite all the multiplication tables in less than two minutes. Matthew said he'd work backward and launched into the twelve-times table, speaking loudly so that Toby could hear above the singing. Brandon and Jason clapped a steady beat to accompany Matthew's recitation.

The telephone rang and the receptionist answered. He said into the mouthpiece, "You'll have to speak up."

Amy told Linh-Mai, "I'll show you a hand-clapping routine." She held her hands in front of her and started, "Miss Mary Mack, Mack, Mack, All dressed in black, black, black …"

Edison said, "Excuse me," and pushed past Steve.

The twins had reached the chorus, "All night long — yeah, yeah. Rock me all night long." They danced as they sang, with Julie and Shay imitating their movements. Matthew was on the nine-times table, his voice getting louder and faster. Amy said, "Let's start again. Miss Mary Mack, Mack, Mack, All dressed in black, black, black …"

Steve followed Edison inside, saying, "Watch who you're shoving."

Edison raised his voice above the commotion. "What *is* your problem?"

"*You're* the problem. You — taking my place and screwing up."

The receptionist said into the telephone, "Hold on." He covered the mouthpiece and shouted, "Will you stupid kids be quiet!"

At the same time Mr. Grease appeared in the doorway. The receptionist watched him nervously as he crossed the little office and leaned on the counter.

"He's with us," said Mr. Field. "He looks after the kids. He makes sure they're treated right, and stuff like that."

The receptionist put down the phone. "Why don't

I find you alternative accommodation?" He worked at his computer for a few minutes, then said, "I've found rooms at the Shanklin Bay Carleton. It's downtown on the waterfront."

★ ★ ★

Edison felt at home in downtown Shanklin Bay. With the city's big malls, tall office buildings, carefully tended parks, and wide streets filled with cars and buses and taxis, it was like being back in Canterbury.

He felt even more at home when they found the hotel. Mr. Grease stopped under an awning that extended from the roadside to the wide glass doors of the entrance. A uniformed attendant opened the van door and said, "Welcome to the Shanklin Bay Carleton."

As they entered, Amy gasped, "This isn't a hotel. It's a *palace*."

It was like the hotels Edison had stayed at when he was travelling with his parents and with elite teams. He took in the gleaming dark wood of the reception desk, the sparkling chandeliers, and the staircase that wound up to a balcony overlooking the foyer.

Toby, stopping to gawk just inside the entrance, his gaze finally settling on the deep pile carpets, said, "Someone keep hold of Linh-Mai, or we'll lose her in the rug."

Mr. Field called the team together. "We have one

room for the girls and two for the boys. Have you thought about how you're going to sleep?"

"What usually does the trick for me is putting my head on the pillow and closing my eyes," said Toby.

Mr. Field rolled his eyes and continued, "I mean, who do you want to share with?"

"You'd better decide," said Shay.

"Okay," said Mr. Field. "Steve, Toby, and Edison share one room, and Shay, Matthew, Jason, and Brandon the other."

Steve opened his mouth as if to protest.

Mr. Field looked at him. "Okay?"

Steve muttered, "I guess."

Mr. Field went on, "We'll meet here in a half hour and walk over to the Shanklin Bay Mall for a couple of hours."

He led the way to the team's rooms, which were side by side on the top floor. The room assigned to Edison, Steve, and Toby contained twin beds, a big television, a desk, two armchairs, and a low cot in a corner.

Toby eyed the cot warily. "That thing doesn't look too comfortable — or safe."

Edison said, "I'll take it."

Toby peered into the bathroom and said, "We could play soccer in here."

Steve was already stretched out on one of the twin beds, the TV remote in his hand. He found "Soccer Round-Up" and said, "This is the life."

"You bet," said Toby. "What do you think, Edison? Ever been in a place like this?"

Edison hesitated. "Well — yes."

"'Course he has," Steve scoffed. "You can't expect superstar soccer players to stay in anything less than five-star hotels, where they have a bunch of people running around after them so they don't have to do anything for themselves. It's like playing soccer when you're a superstar, and everyone on the team is supposed to set you up to score so you look good without actually doing anything."

Edison ignored him, and Steve went on, "Trouble is — when you can't score even then, you end up looking like a useless bonehead." He paused and added, "Isn't that right, Eddie?"

"Shut up," said Edison.

"Who are you telling to shut up?" said Steve, throwing the remote aside and swinging his legs off the bed.

"Whoa, guys," said Toby. "It's time to meet the others."

★ ★ ★

A sign at the entrance to the Shanklin Bay Mall boasted, *Over one hundred stores! Biggest mall in the Maritimes!*

Edison knew there were at least six malls in Canterbury that were bigger, but he didn't say anything.

The mall was crowded and Mr. Field said, "We'll stay together."

Julie said, "But Linh-Mai and Amy and the twins and I want to go in girls' shops."

"That's okay," said Mr. Field. "We'll come with you."

Julie folded her arms. "You're *not* coming in girls' shops with us."

Toby said, "I'd rather someone pulled my toenails out than go in girls' shops."

Mr. Field sighed. "All right, you can go off by yourselves. But stay in two groups — boys and girls — and meet here in two hours. Mr. Grease and I will be in the food court if you need us."

The boys were on their way back to the meeting place when they stopped to look in the window of All-sports Megastore, where a pair of gold-coloured cleats formed the centrepiece of a display of soccer equipment. A sign beside the golden shoes said, *As worn by Rudy Kohler of Real Madrid.*

"I'd like a pair of shoes like that," said Toby. "But I wouldn't use them for soccer. I'd go dancing in them."

"They look like superstar shoes," said Steve.

Edison knew what was coming.

"I expect Eddie would like a pair like that," Steve went on. He looked at Edison. "Eh, Eddie?"

Edison ignored him.

Steve said, "I'm talking to you," and punched him on the shoulder.

Edison put his hand on Steve's chest and pushed him away.

Steve asked, "Who are you pushing?" He stood squarely in front of Edison, his arms by his sides and his fists clenched.

Toby pushed between them. "Guys, knock it off! What's up with you, Steve? Edison hasn't done anything to you."

Steve answered, "No?"

★ ★ ★

In the morning, when they went down to breakfast, they were met at the restaurant door by a babble of voices. A group of students was sitting at a long table in the corner. The adult with them, a young woman with short black hair and big hooped earrings, waved them over and said, "Why don't you join us?"

Her students, smiling and beckoning, moved their chairs so that the two groups mingled around the table. Edison found himself near Mr. Field and the young woman, who was saying, "I'm Casey. Where are you from?"

Mr. Field said, "Brunswick Valley. We're a soccer team."

"So are we. We're here for the provincial Special Olympics soccer tournament." Casey waved a hand toward her group. "Meet the Dorchester All Stars."

Mr. Field said, "We're on tour, and we play our last game in Dorchester — against High Park Memorial Academy."

Casey pulled a face. "You'd better be in top form. They take soccer very seriously. They'll know all about you and your team before you even arrive. I know because I was at school in Dorchester and we used to play High Park. I was friends with a boy on the team, and he told me High Park sends someone to watch its opponents' games and make notes on the players."

As he followed the conversation, Edison was nodding without realizing it.

Mr. Field said, "Do you know about that sort of thing, Edison?"

He murmured, "Yes."

He remembered a coach at an elite training camp showing him something called a player profile and warning, "Every team you play against has a dossier like this — on you." He'd been allowed to read his own player profile. The strengths it listed — his speed, his ability to dribble past defenders, his powerful shooting — didn't surprise him. But the paragraph that followed, outlining his weaknesses, had been a shock. *For all his ability, Edison Flood lacks confidence. He is easily intimidated, and if put under pressure is likely to lose his nerve.*

Edison had been about to take a mouthful of cereal. He paused, his spoon midway between the bowl and his mouth. He lowered his spoon.

Why hadn't he remembered the profile? Now he knew why he was choking at crucial moments in his games.

He'd lost his nerve.

But why?

The profile said "easily intimidated." Had he been intimidated into losing his confidence and his nerve? He couldn't remember any particular act of intimidation that might have caused it, but he recalled lots of little incidents that referees had missed, times he'd been tripped, pushed in the back, held back by his shirt, elbowed off the ball. He wondered whether all these incidents had gradually drained away his confidence, because every one of them had made him appear weak.

But the profile said he was likely to lose his nerve "if put under pressure."

Maybe it wasn't intimidation that had caused him to lose his nerve, but pressure. He tried to remember how he'd felt at his moments of choking, when he'd failed to shoot in that last game for the Eagles, and when he'd had only Lily to beat, and when he'd had the open goal against Centreville. Was it pressure he'd felt then?

He turned his attention back to Casey, who was saying, "High Park is a very tough team. And what makes them even tougher to play is they get huge support for all their games. Do you have supporters with you?"

Mr. Field shook his head.

"The support their team gets can blow you right off

the field." She grinned. "Perhaps I'll bring the Dorchester All Stars to cheer for you."

A little girl with a round face and a snub nose, her hair standing up around her head in a wild frizzy halo, was sitting opposite Edison, staring at him.

He said, "What?"

"Who are you?"

"I'm Edison."

"Why?"

"I don't know." He leaned forward to read the sticker on her sweater. It said, *Hello! I'm Ella.* "Why are you Ella?"

She smiled and nodded. "Ella."

She resumed staring at Edison, who asked, hoping to divert her intense gaze, "Do you like playing soccer?"

She grinned and nodded. "Play soccer!"

"I bet you win all your games."

Ella frowned. "Don't get you."

Edison said, faltering, "You know, win — when you score more goals than the other team."

Ella shook her head, still frowning.

Casey, who'd been listening, said, "We like playing soccer — right, Ella?"

"Play soccer!"

"And scoring goals …"

"Score goals — yeah!"

Casey added to Edison, "But we don't talk about winning or losing. We just talk about playing, and enjoying the game."

"No pressure, eh?" said Mr. Field, catching Edison's eye.

After breakfast, the two teams met on the board-walk behind the hotel. Ella sought out Edison, seizing his hand and clinging to it, as the two groups wandered along the waterfront trail, looking at fishing boats set-ting out from the wharf and the ferry easing into the terminal. They counted seals in the harbour, looking for the sleek shiny heads bobbing up above the water.

At the end of the trail, Casey and the Dorchester All Stars caught a bus back to the hotel to prepare for their tournament, while Mr. Grease met the Brunswick Valley team to take them on to the Shanklin Bay Mu-seum.

Two hours later, as they drove out of the city, they passed the recreation grounds where the Dorchester All Stars were playing, and Mr. Field said, "We have time to watch for ten minutes."

Four games were in progress, and the field was a riot of colour and sound as the Special Olympics teams, in their bright uniforms, darted and wheeled after the ball, whooping and laughing all the time. Edison and his friends found the Dorchester All Stars and joined Casey on the sideline. Edison quickly picked out Ella, her face wearing a constant smile and her eyes shining with excitement. She saw Edison and flew across the field to hug him. She gasped, "Love soccer," and rushed back to the game. When her side scored, her teammates danced and cheered, and when the other side scored a few minutes later, they danced and cheered just as enthusiastically.

Mr. Field, glancing at his watch, said, "We have to get on to North Bay." As the Brunswick Valley team headed back to the van, with a final wave to the All Stars, Casey called, "Enjoy your game!" and her team stopped playing in order to wave and repeat, "Enjoy your game!"

Edison tried to ignore the flutters of anxiety he felt at the mention of the game ahead. He supposed it helped to know you were choking because you'd lost your nerve.

But how did you get it back?

7 NORTH BAY

Although North Bay was only a few kilometres north of Shanklin Bay, it seemed a world away. The streets, wide and laid in a grid pattern, were deserted. Edison stared at abandoned gas stations, boarded up stores, and playgrounds with broken, rusting equipment. The houses were identical, little boxes in yards that contained a patch of lank grass, a snarling dog chained to a battered kennel, a discarded refrigerator, or a car on blocks. Many of them were empty, their windows smashed.

On Grand Parade, where a sign said *Business District*, a group of men standing outside Bubba's Bar and Grill scowled as the van went by. One leaned to spit deliberately. The post office was boarded up, and a sign outside a church said *For Sale*.

"This place gives me the creeps," said Linh-Mai. "It's like a ghost town."

Mr. Field turned in his seat. "It's a mining town, but the mine closed two years ago. Now it's a noth-

67

ing town. People want to move away because there's nothing to stay for, but they can't sell their houses because there's nothing for people to come here for, so they're stuck."

North Bay Regional School was at the end of a road leading off Grand Parade, tucked under a wall of rock that rose steeply behind the town. A group of high-school students shooting baskets stopped when they saw the van. On the field beside the school, a soccer team in grey shirts and black shorts was warming up.

A woman with a tired face and flowing black hair streaked with grey approached the van as they climbed out. "I'm the coach. You're late. Let's get started."

Edison changed quickly and jogged around the field while he waited for the rest of the team. The now-familiar foreboding was settling over him like a clinging web. He sprinted, hoping to shake it off by making his pulse race through exertion rather than through anxiety. If only he could relax, he thought, maybe he could control the nerves that crippled him on the field.

He went into his usual warm-up routine. By the time he was running backward across the field, he found most of his teammates alongside him.

"We thought we might play better if we did the same warm-up as you," Linh-Mai explained.

When they stopped to focus and envisage, Edison tried to imagine scoring, but all he saw was himself choking and missing open goals.

Mr. Field called the team together. "We'll play 4–4–2. Steve and Edison, see if you can bang in a few goals, eh? That's all. Just go play."

The North Bay players were finishing their warm-up with shooting practice, and a tall red-headed girl was firing fierce shots at goal. The high-school students who had been playing basketball had sauntered across to the field and one of the North Bay players, a broad squat boy who looked older than his teammates, had joined them. North Bay lined up for the start and, as he rejoined his team, the students shouted, "Kill 'em, Beast." When Brunswick Valley lined up, one shouted, "You're going to get a kicking from the Beast." Mr. Grease wandered over to them and they scattered toward the basketball court.

Steve took the kickoff and tapped the ball to Edison, who passed back to Julie and set off toward the North Bay goal with Steve. Julie passed to Shay, who dribbled upfield. Steve positioned himself on one side of the penalty area, where the Beast and another North Bay defender jostled him. Edison moved wide of the goal on the other side, and two defenders moved with him. As he watched Shay looking for one of his strikers to pass to, Edison found himself keeping at least one defender in the way, making it impossible for Shay to pass to him safely. He was hardly aware of doing it until Shay passed to Steve. Despite being hemmed in by his

markers — the Beast elbowing him and the other holding his shirt — Steve got the ball. Now Edison knew
he should run into the space closer to the goal where
Steve would send the ball. But he hesitated — just long
enough for one of the defenders to reach Steve's pass
before he did. Even now he could still tackle the defender, try to rob him of the ball and get a shot at goal,
or at least block the clearance he was about to make.
But again he hung back. As the defender cleared, at the
same time as Edison moved too late to challenge, Edison saw what he was doing.

He was avoiding the action, because doing nothing
was better than screwing up. It wasn't something he'd
planned. It just seemed to happen.

"Jeez, Edison," Steve shouted. "Get stuck in."

Edison nodded an apology and ran back to help his
defence.

With North Bay on the attack most of the time, he
hovered between Brunswick Valley's goal area and midfield. Several times he weaved around opponents, when
he was sure he could beat them, but was careful not to
get in a position where his teammates would expect
him to shoot.

Only once in the first half did Edison find himself
with a scoring chance, when Toby broke up a North
Bay attack and punted the ball out to Jillian. She passed
ahead to Steve, who set off down the wing. The Beast
charged in from the side and Steve swung toward him.

They crashed together and Steve's head jolted back as the Beast's flailing arm caught him under the chin, but he scrambled the ball past him and kept going. Two more defenders ran out to block his path, leaving Edison unmarked. Steve rounded the first defender, but the second jumped in front of him and met him sideways, so that Steve's face smashed into his shoulder. As Steve reeled back, clutching his nose, the ball rolled between where the goalkeeper crouched on his line and where Edison waited. Edison thought he could beat the keeper to the ball and stab it into the net. But the keeper might get there first. Or Edison might get the ball and miss the empty net.

He hesitated for a fraction of a second — so short a time he was sure only he would be aware he could have moved faster — before launching himself forward. The goalkeeper dived on the ball and Edison jumped over him.

Steve sneered, "Scared of getting dirty, Mr. Superstar?"

Edison knew it was his fault Brunswick Valley had wasted a scoring chance. But it wasn't just his fault. The midfielders should have been following up and one of them could also have tried for goal. Instead, they'd been strung across the field in perfect formation, as if they were more concerned with looking good than with hustling for the ball.

At halftime, Mr. Field said, "Relax, guys. Play your

usual game. Run and hustle."

But the second half started the same way, with Brunswick Valley keeping formation and passing carefully to keep possession, without ever managing to mount any threatening attacks. The North Bay players, on the other hand, seemed to be holding in reserve the ability to strike when they chose. The red-headed girl quickly fired off a couple of shots at goal. Amy saved the first one easily, but was caught out of position by the second and just managed to scramble it away with her feet. When North Bay won a corner kick, the Beast positioned himself in front of Amy. She backed away but he moved with her. The ball sailed across the goalmouth. When Amy tried to jump for it, he stepped backward onto her cleats, anchoring her to the ground, while the ball fell to the red-headed striker, who shot into the net.

As Brunswick Valley pressed for an equalizer, North Bay dropped back into two lines of five players strung across the field to block every attack. Edison, looking at his teammates, thought, *They're playing too carefully*. He corrected himself: *We're playing too carefully*. But he couldn't bring himself to break out of his caution. He was too afraid of choking. It was better to play it safe.

Only Steve was playing with the frenzy Edison had seen in the casual practice game at school. When Linh-Mai made a long clearance for Steve to collect and run at goal, the Beast elbowed him off the ball.

Steve fell, but picked himself up and gave chase. He caught up with his opponent on the edge of the penalty area. As he moved in to tackle, the Beast swung his arm sideways, hitting Steve in the eye. Steve moved in again and this time managed to poke the ball free. He fired it at the goal just before the Beast crashed into him, flattening him. The surprised goalkeeper didn't move as the ball cannonaded off a goalpost and bounced toward Edison. Edison looked at the referee, expecting him to call a foul on Steve, but the ref waved play on. Before Edison moved toward the loose ball, a defender cleared.

Edison heard Steve give a disgusted snort.

With only minutes left in the game, Edison was resigned to defeat. He thought he'd got through the game without appearing to choke, but he certainly hadn't helped his teammates when he probably could have won the game for them. He didn't know what made him more ashamed — choking or playing it safe.

Then the North Bay goalkeeper let the ball slip from his hand as he attempted a long throw out. It hit one of the fullbacks who was standing nearby and bounced back toward the net. The goalkeeper and the fullback fell over one another, and the ball trickled into the net.

When the game ended with the score level, Mr. Field greeted his team with, "We got lucky."

"I guess so," said Shay with a wry grin.

"Why were you playing so carefully, all of you? Why

didn't you play your usual game? I said to just go play, and to run and hustle."

Shay looked around at his teammates. "It didn't seem right, scrambling and hustling after the ball, like we were in a fool-around practice game. Now we're champions — sort of — we should look like champions, shouldn't we?"

"You should look like yourselves. And play like yourselves. We won our division because we played with such zest and fun. Now it's almost like we've forgotten how to enjoy our game." He surveyed the serious faces of his team and added, "Come on, guys. It's not the end of the world. Let's try to play our old game against Long Island tomorrow."

"We'll have to play better — now that we have to win the next two games," said Shay.

"That's *all* of us play better," Steve muttered with a glance at Edison, who was standing at the edge of the group, leaning against the van. Steve's shirt and shorts were covered in mud, and his knees were red and raw from the falls he'd taken. His nose had a crust of blood under it, and his forehead and eye were bruised. Edison's knees were clean, and his shorts and shirt looked as if they'd just come out of the wash.

Edison turned away and rested his head on the side window, glad of the cool glass against his forehead.

Mr. Grease, who'd been cleaning the windshield, walked around to him and said, "Okay?"

Edison nodded.

Mr. Grease grunted. After a pause, he nodded at Mr. Field. "Ask him about pressure." He grunted again and returned to his window cleaning.

By the time the team had changed and were climbing in the van, everyone seemed to be regaining their good spirits. The twins were chattering excitedly about Long Island.

"We used to live there," Jillian announced for the third time.

"Until we were five," said Jessica.

"You mean, until last year?" said Toby.

Jillian said, "Ha ha."

Edison pulled the tour itinerary from his pocket. They were staying at the Wharfside Motel in Back Harbour tonight, so they could get the first ferry in the morning to Long Island. He wondered what the Wharfside Motel was like, and whether he'd have to share a room with Toby and Steve again. He didn't mind sharing with Toby, but he was sick of Steve sniping at him.

Hardly anyone spoke as they drove through the bleak streets of North Bay and headed south on the highway. From the corner of his eye Edison could see Shay already asleep, and soon Julie dozed off, leaning against him. Toby and Amy were talking quietly on the back seat, and he thought the twins were sharing a book, because he could hear pages turning.

Two hours later, as Mr. Grease pulled into the Wharfside Motel, Mr. Field said, "Lights out at ten, and no noise after that. Share rooms like before."

8 ON THE WHARF

The Wharfside Motel consisted of a row of connected cabins with a restaurant at one end. The cabin Edison was sharing with Steve and Toby contained two single beds, a blow-up mattress on the floor, and a closet-sized bathroom. It had one little window that looked across the road to the open sea. Edison said he'd take the mattress. It meant he'd be further from Steve. As he lay on it, he could hear Shay, Matthew, Jason, and Brandon in the cabin on one side, and the girls in the cabin on the other. At first he thought their voices were coming through the thin walls, but then he realized he was hearing them through the heating vent in the floor beside his mattress.

There was a knock at the door and Mr. Field peered in. "I have messages for Toby and Edison." He consulted a note in his hand. "Toby, your mother says you're allowed to take something for seasickness tomorrow if you want. She's just found the permission slip I sent home with you."

Toby made a tutting sound. "She's always losing things."

"She says she found it when she was cleaning your room. That was the first she'd seen of it."

"Really?" said Toby innocently. "How strange."

"Would you like a couple of my pills?"

"Nah, thanks," Toby said confidently. "I don't need them."

Mr. Field looked at another note. "Edison, your mother says she'll be at High Park to watch the game." He looked up. "That's good. We'll need all the support we can get against the Academy." He glanced back at his notes. "Nothing for you, Steve."

"Figures," said Steve.

When Mr. Field had gone, Steve asked Edison, "Why's your ma coming to watch us play High Park?"

"Dunno."

"Why didn't she watch us play Centreville and North Bay?"

Edison shrugged.

"Why just High Park?" Steve persisted. "Are you trying to get in there or something?"

Edison didn't answer.

Steve, who was lying on one of the beds, raised himself on one elbow and said slowly, "That's it, isn't it? Your ma's going to get you into High Park."

"You don't just get into High Park," said Edison. "You have to try out."

"Like you'll have to try out, coming from Canterbury, and with your folks knowing who to talk to so they get you in."

"My coach at Canterbury recommended me, and the sports director at High Park said our game with them could count as my trial. All right?"

Steve snorted and flung himself down on the bed with his face to the wall.

Toby put on the TV and lay on his bed watching a game show, while Edison settled back on his mattress and closed his eyes. He was sick of being needled by Steve, but he had only two more days to put up with it. That was how many hours? It was nine-thirty, Sunday night, and they'd be home around five-thirty on Tuesday night, so that made twenty-four hours until this time tomorrow, and another two-and-a-half until it was Tuesday, and then ...

He must have dozed off. The TV was still on, but Toby was in the bathroom. Steve hadn't moved. He seemed to be asleep. Edison glanced at the clock on the wall. Ten minutes until lights out. Ten more minutes to put up with Steve. He decided to spend them outside, in case Steve woke and started at him again. He slipped outside and closed the door quietly behind him.

He could make out the open sea on the other side of a wall of rocks across the road. A few steps beyond the motel, the road ended where the wharf began. A cluster of lights illuminated the far end where the ferry came in, and a few more lights spaced out along the dock threw pools of light. It was raining and the wind was picking up. He could hear the slap of waves against the sea wall, and his face was growing sticky with the salty spray that the wind was flinging across the road.

"You make me sick."

Edison turned. Steve was standing in the cabin doorway.

"Get lost." He set off toward the wharf.

Steve followed, saying, "You're a total screw-up, but it won't matter, will it? You'll still walk into High Park."

Edison spoke over his shoulder. "What's it to you, anyway?"

"I tried out for High Park and they turned me down."

Edison remembered the Eagles coach saying someone from Brunswick Valley had tried out for the Academy. So it had been Steve. "That's not my fault."

"You ought to know what sort of place you're getting in to."

"What's that supposed to mean?"

"Do you want to know why I didn't get in?"

They were on the wharf, in the darkness between two pools of light. The choppy sea glistened beyond the low wooden barrier at the edge of the wharf. It was raining heavily.

Edison stopped, his back to Steve. "I don't give a

toss why you didn't get in."

"I'll tell you anyway. I had a trial, and I got in. Then two days later it was, 'oh, sorry. On reflection we've decided you're unsuitable for High Park.' So Mr. Field bugged them for a reason, and guess what they told him about why I didn't get in."

"I told you already. I don't care."

Steve repeated, his voice rising as he spat the words, "Guess what they told him. They said I was unsuitable because I had inadequate parental support. Translation: We found out your old man's inside and that means you and your folks aren't good enough for us."

"That's not my problem."

"Wrong." Steve jabbed Edison in the shoulder. "It's your problem because screw-ups like you get into High Park without even trying and that means there's no room for me."

"That's crazy."

"Right — but it's true."

"It's not my fault. Leave me alone."

"Why don't you make me?"

Edison stared at the lights at the end of the wharf.

Steve jabbed him on the shoulder again. "Why don't you make me?"

Edison raised his elbow and swung around, catching Steve on the jaw. As Steve staggered backward, Edison turned and pushed him hard on the chest with both hands. Steve grabbed Edison as he fell and pulled him down with him, smashing his face against the boards of the wharf. Edison half raised himself. He thought his nose was bleeding, although it was hard to say if it was blood or rain running into his mouth. He felt Steve's knee on his back, forcing him down. He lashed out with his arm, catching Steve on the side of the head, and squirmed free. He scrambled up.

Heavy feet sounded on the wharf, approaching at a run.

Edison rushed at Steve and they staggered backwards.

"Jeez, guys. Knock it off." It was Toby's voice. "Guys, quit it!"

Their feet hit the low board at the edge of the wharf and they flew into the air. The last thing Edison heard before he hit the water was Toby's voice from above them.

"*Jeez*, guys. Now what am I supposed to do?"

9 SHARED UNDERSTANDING

"How are we going to get our clothes dry?" asked Steve. Edison, Steve, and Toby were in their Brunswick Valley School soccer outfits. They had changed into them as soon as they got back to the cabin. Their sodden clothes lay in a pile in the middle of the floor, and a trail of wet footprints led from the door to Toby's bed where they sat. They had turned the heat up as high as it would go.

"Let's ask the girls," said Toby. "They know about stuff like that."

"We can't risk going round to their cabin," said Steve. "We're lucky we got back here without Mr. Field seeing us."

Edison and Steve had still been floundering from the shock of their fall into the frigid water when there had been a huge splash between them. Toby, standing up to his chest in water, had grabbed each of them by the collar, hauled them to their feet, and ordered, "No more fighting. And no drowning."

Edison had looked at Steve and said, "Jerk." Steve

said, "Freakin' idiot." Then, suddenly, they were laughing, all three of them, as Toby marched them to the shore beside the wharf and they scrambled up to the road.

"I know how to ask the girls," said Edison. He lay on the floor with his head beside the heater vent. He tapped, and spoke into it. "Is anyone awake in there?"

There was no response. He tapped louder. "Anyone awake?"

He heard a mutter of voices from next door. Then, a few seconds later, Julie's voice said, "Go away."

Edison looked at Toby and Steve.

Toby said, "Try again."

Edison tapped louder.

"I said, go away."

Edison tapped louder still.

"We're asleep."

"No, you're not."

"We were."

"Sorry."

"Bug off."

Edison tapped even louder.

Julie swore — Edison was surprised at the word she used — and snapped, "Who is it?"

"Edison."

"What do you want?"

"Help."

"So? We've got a big game tomorrow, in case you've

84

forgotten, and you might want to stay up all night but we're trying to sleep …"

"Tell her to shut up," said Toby.

Edison said, "Shut up and listen."

There was a pause, then, "Don't tell me to shut up, you snot-nosed bonehead."

Edison looked at Toby and Steve. They were grinning.

Toby whispered, "You should hear her when she gets mad."

Edison tried again, speaking more urgently. "We need help."

"What sort of help?"

"Come round and we'll tell you."

"You come round here."

"Can't."

A few seconds later, after another murmuring of voices, Julie and Linh-Mai stole into the boys' cabin. Linh-Mai was wearing Spiderman pajamas, and Julie had on a long T-shirt with a picture of a wrestler on the front. He had a square shaven head and a drooping moustache, and his open, snarling mouth revealed three missing teeth.

"Nice sleepwear," said Toby. "It's clever how they can put your picture on your T-shirt, isn't it?"

Julie smacked him on the side of his head. She had been surveying the boys in their Brunswick Valley uniforms and said, "It's a bit late for playing soccer, isn't it?"

Then her eyes fell on the pile of wet clothes. "What's going on?"

"We went swimming," said Steve.

"In your clothes," said Julie.

"We forgot to take them off," said Toby.

"And now you want us to get them dry," said Linh-Mai. She looked at Julie. "Why are boys so useless?"

She crept from the cabin and returned a few seconds later with two hair dryers.

Julie said, "We're not helping until you tell us what really happened."

While the boys held up their wet clothes and the girls wielded the dryers, Toby started, "Steve and Edison got into it."

"Why doesn't that surprise me?" said Julie.

"He started it," said Steve. "Boasting about going to High Park …"

"You're the one that started on about High Park," said Edison.

"Don't start again," said Toby.

Linh-Mai looked at Edison. "You're going to *High Park*?"

"Don't know yet."

"'Course you know," said Steve. "That's the only reason you're playing for us — just so you can show off when we play them."

Julie and Linh-Mai were looking at Edison.

He gnawed at his lip. "My old coach at Canterbury recommended me to High Park," he started.

"That means he's in," said Steve.

"Let him finish," said Julie.

"The High Park coach said I had to try out, but if I played for Brunswick Valley when they played High Park that could count as my trial."

"So he's in," said Steve.

"Not unless I play better," said Edison. He hung his head. "Right now I'm pathetic."

"If High Park had turned me down because I wasn't good enough, I wouldn't have minded," said Steve bitterly. "But when it's because of ..." He stopped, shaking his head, and swore softly.

Toby put his hand on Steve's shoulder. "It's not fair, about your dad and all," he said. "But that's not Edison's fault."

Steve muttered, "I guess." After a few seconds of silence, he said suddenly, looking at Edison, "You'll be all right. You've just lost your nerve."

Edison looked up in surprise. "How did you know?"

"Obvious, isn't it? Don't worry. You'll get it back, all of a sudden. You just have to keep trying."

"What do you mean, he's lost his nerve?" said Linh-Mai. "What's he talking about, Edison?"

"Like Steve says, I've lost my nerve," said Edison. "You can't play soccer — you can't play *any* sport — if you've lost your nerve."

Julie and Linh-Mai and Toby were looking from Edison to Steve, their faces blank.

Steve explained, "You have to, like, *know* that whatever you plan to do — shoot, or dribble, or whatever — you're going to do."

"If you don't believe it, you might as well not bother," said Edison.

Steve nodded.

"How d'you mean?" asked Toby.

"I mean, it takes nerve to try to play ... like Steve and I do ..." He was afraid of sounding conceited and spoke hesitantly. "Trying to dribble round defenders — that takes nerve. If you do a step-over, or a feint, or whatever, and you get past them, you look great, right? But when your stuff doesn't work and they get the ball off you, then you just look stupid."

Linh-Mai interrupted, "No, you don't."

"You do," Steve insisted. "And trying a shot at goal — that takes nerve too."

"Can't say I've ever tried it," said Toby.

"You're a hero if you score," said Edison. "But more likely the goalkeeper's going to save ..."

"... Or someone's going to block your shot," said Steve.

"... Or you miss," said Edison.

"So you end up looking a complete loser," Steve concluded.

"Not just a loser," Edison added. "A cocky show-off loser."

Steve nodded again.

"Jeez," said Toby. "Missing a goal isn't the end of the world."

"You guys are so totally heavy," said Julie. "Lighten up, will you? We're playing soccer, not … not … waging war."

Steve looked at Edison. "They don't know what it's like, do they?"

Edison said softly, "No."

Julie started, "So you two got in an argument about soccer, and …" She looked scornfully at Edison and Steve. "Don't tell me you got in a fight over it."

Edison looked at Steve, who looked at Edison. They hung their heads.

"What a couple of jerks," said Julie.

"It wasn't really a fight," said Edison.

"It was just a sort of push … or two," said Steve.

"Then we fell off the wharf," said Edison.

"And Toby jumped in after us," said Steve.

"He was like a Newfoundland dog swimming to the rescue," said Edison.

"More like a rescue hippopotamus," Toby put in. "Anyway, I can't swim."

Edison and Steve and the girls looked at him in astonishment.

"But … what if it had been deep?" said Steve. "Like, too deep to stand?"

Toby shrugged. "I didn't think of that."

Edison started, "Toby …" Then he couldn't think what to say.

Linh-Mai broke the silence. "It's like a sauna in here."

"We didn't want to end up dead of hypothermia," Toby explained.

"We'll all be dead anyway if Mr. Field catches us," said Julie. "He'll send us home."

"We'd better get back to our cabin," said Linh-Mai. "Your clothes aren't quite dry, but they will be by morning."

Edison, Steve, and Toby whispered, "Thanks, girls."

"Where would you be without us?" said Julie as she slipped out of the door after Linh-Mai.

10 LONG ISLAND

Edison woke to the sound of the twins' excited voices outside the cabin door. He peered through the little window. Wind and rain were lashing the cabin and, across the road, sheets of spray were shooting into the air as waves thudded against the sea wall. The twins, in bright yellow raincoats, were facing the spray, laughing as it landed on their upturned faces. Julie, Amy, and Linh-Mai came out and joined them.

Julie banged on the boys' door and shouted, "Wake up in there."

"Go away," Toby called, pulling the bedclothes over his head.

"They have great breakfasts here," said Jillian.

"I'll be right out," said Toby, scrambling out of bed.

The boys dressed quickly and ran to the café, where they sat with the girls.

"What's the special?" Toby asked.

"Eggs and bacon …" Jessica started.

"And sausages …" Jillian continued.

"With beans and home fries," Jessica finished.

"Bring it on," said Toby.

Edison, listening to the roar of the wind, said, "I'll have a piece of toast."

Toby had nearly finished his breakfast when a particularly fierce gust of wind shook the café, and a wall of spray slammed against it.

Jessica said, "It's going to be fun on the ferry."

Edison asked nervously, "Will it be rough?"

"It depends what you mean by rough," said Jillian.

"And on the direction of the wind," Jessica added. "If it's blowing north–south it's not too bad, because the ferry slices through the swell with just a backward and forward rocking motion …"

Toby, taking a last mouthful, paused and echoed uncertainly, "Backward and forward rocking motion?"

"… But if the wind is blowing east–west, across the boat, you get this *really* fun backward and forward *and* side to side rocking motion," Jillian went on.

The twins, giggling, demonstrated.

Toby murmured weakly, "Backward and forward *and* side to side?"

Edison asked, "Which way is the wind blowing?"

The twins glanced through the window at the flag flapping wildly in front of the motel. Jillian said, "Looks like east–west."

Toby groaned.

Mr. Field was consulting a list. "Those of you whose

parents sent in permission slips for you to take seasickness pills, you'd better take them now."

Edison took the pills his mother had given him. Everyone else, except the twins and Toby, did the same.

Toby approached Mr. Field and started, "About those pills …"

"… You've changed your mind," Mr. Field finished for him. He held out two pills. "Have you taken seasickness pills before?"

Toby shook his head.

Mr. Field consulted the side of the carton. "It says here side effects can be drowsiness, lack of concentration, and loss of mental and physical coordination. In other words, it can make you so you're only half aware of what's going on around you, and you just want to sit and stare."

"Like being in math class," said Toby.

"You can't fool around with this stuff," Mr. Field warned. "You never know how you're going to react to medication. Get your friends to keep an eye on you."

Toby took the pills and followed the others out, while Mr. Field said quietly to Edison, "You're not happy with how you're playing, are you?"

Edison shook his head. "I've lost my nerve."

"I know. Usually that means you feel under pressure, and that means you have to ask where the pressure is coming from."

"It's like everyone expects me to play well all the time."

"Everyone?"

"My coaches …"

"Me?"

"Well, no. But all my other coaches, and … and … my mother."

"Your mother wants what's best for you."

"She wants me to go to High Park."

"I know. She told me before you arrived."

"Is that all right? Playing for Brunswick Valley so I can try out against High Park?"

"Of course, but do *you* want to go to High Park?"

Edison realized he'd never really thought about it. "I don't know."

"Talk to your mother about it. Tell her you feel under pressure."

"Mr. Grease said to ask you about pressure."

"He did, eh?" Mr. Field paused before going on. "My father is Dan Field."

"Dan Field who used to play soccer for Canada? Your father is *Dan Field*?"

"That's what everybody says when I tell them. And when I used to play soccer — serious soccer — that's who everybody expected me to be. But I'm not Dan Field. I was never as good as my dad, for a start, although it took me a while to accept that."

"What did you do?"

"I gave up serious soccer."

"Are you saying I should give up serious soccer if I

can't handle how people expect me to play?"

"I'm saying you have to decide why you want to play serious soccer. Is it because someone — your coaches, or your mother, or whoever — expects you to? Are you playing to fulfill someone else's expectations? Or are you playing simply because you love soccer?"

Edison said, "I love soccer, but …"

"But nothing. Just enjoy the game."

While Mr. Grease put the van in the lineup for the ferry, the team waited on the wharf, sheltering from the pouring rain and ducking showers of spray as they watched the ferry dock. When they boarded, Toby sat on a bench at the front, facing out to sea.

"You'll get wet," Edison warned.

"Is it raining?" said Toby.

Edison and Steve went on a tour of the boat. In the lounge, crew members were chaining tables and chairs to the floor. The twins were flying from table to table, greeting and hugging old friends. As the ferry pulled away from the wharf with a long blast on its horn, the boys raced out on deck to gaze in the direction of Long Island, although the twins had told them it wouldn't come into sight until the ferry was clear of the rocky outcrop that guarded the mouth of the harbour. Mr. Grease was leaning on the rail, watching the wharf slip away. Edison and Steve stood on each side of him. He smiled as the ferry lurched wildly when it reached open water.

Edison said, "Where's Mr. Field?"

Mr. Grease grinned and jerked his thumb over his shoulder at the window of the lounge. Edison looked in and saw Mr. Field lying on a bench, his eyes closed.

"I think I'll do the same," Steve said uncertainly as the ferry lurched again.

Edison headed for the front to check on Toby. He found him smiling happily as the bow dipped into the waves one second and reared up the next, sending sheets of spray over him.

Edison said, "Are you okay?"

Toby nodded, smiling blissfully.

"Are you sure you're not having a reaction to the seasickness pills?"

"I'm not complaining," said Toby, still smiling.

As he spoke, Mr. Grease strolled around the corner. He looked critically at Toby and told Edison, "I'll watch him."

Feeling his stomach churn, Edison retreated to the lounge, where Steve and Shay were leaning back in their seats, their eyes closed. Julie staggered in, sat beside Shay for a moment, then rose and said, "I may as well stay in the bathroom."

Two hours later, when the ferry nosed alongside the wharf on Long Island, the rain had stopped and the wind was dying down. Edison found Toby and told him, "We've arrived. We're tied up at the wharf."

"That was the best ride of my life," said Toby.

Mr. Grease followed the line of ferry traffic through a huddle of cottages at the end of the wharf and onto the single island road. They passed several busy wharves before coming to the school, which consisted of a low building with two wings forming a courtyard sheltered from the wind and the sea. The soccer field lay behind the school, and beyond it was the sea. A crowd of islanders of all ages applauded when Mr. Grease stopped in front of the school.

A woman with a square face and jaw and short coppery hair strode forward. "Welcome to Long Island. I'm the coach, Hannah Guptill. We have a surprise for you — a lunch in honour of your visit!"

She threw open the door of the school and the smell of fish chowder wafted out. Edison held his breath while Steve turned away, his hand to his mouth, and Shay stifled a groan. Julie ran behind a clump of alders and threw up.

"Great," said Toby. "I'm starving."

Mr. Field said weakly, "That's very kind."

Hannah Guptill took his arm and led him inside. The twins broke free of the hugs they were receiving from their old friends and followed them. Edison wondered if it would be rude to refuse the meal.

The Long Island team served lunch. Edison sipped listlessly at his soup, trying to avoid the slimier bits of chowder, as he watched Mr. Grease finish three bowls, and the twins two each. Across the table, Toby dreamily spooned chowder into his mouth, hardly noticing when an empty bowl was removed and a full one put down in its place.

Edison was one of the first to leave the table. He ventured out by himself to the field. The sun had come out and the wind was now a gentle breeze that riffled the sea into a series of sparkling troughs stretching to the horizon. A stack of lobster traps beside the field had toppled over and grass was growing through them. Beyond the field, boats were pulled up on the shingled beach and nets were laid out to dry.

As players from both sides drifted out to the field, the twins introduced some of their old friends to the Brunswick Valley team.

Jessica said, "This is Cousin Buddy." The Long Island centre forward waved.

Jillian pointed to another forward. "This is Junior Green."

"And here's Cousin Rachel," said Jessica, flinging her arm around one of the island midfielders.

When Hannah Guptill called the Long Island team together, the Brunswick Valley players gathered around Mr. Field.

"How shall we play?" Shay asked.

Mr. Field waved them away. "Just go play. Have fun."

Edison wondered how they were going to play an important game when most of them could hardly stand up. He'd forgotten about focusing and envisaging, but it didn't seem to matter. As he listened to the waves rattling the pebble beach, and felt the rough grass under his feet, he reflected on what a contrast the Long Island soccer field was to the grounds he used to play on. The contrast was not just in the surroundings, the pitch, and the way Mr. Field coached, but also in the carefree way his new friends played, the way he'd decided he was going to try to play.

He stood close to Steve for the kickoff, and Steve said, "I'm going to throw up if I run."

Edison said, "I'll try to get in positions for you to pass without moving too much."

"Remember what I said," Steve urged. "Keep trying — and you'll get your nerve back."

When the game started, Edison felt as if he was playing in slow motion. Every thought and action was an effort as he tried to shake off the effects of the ferry ride. He could tell that his friends were in even worse shape. Steve was still on the halfway line, while Julie and Shay were moving even less. Whenever the play allowed, they stood bent over with their hands resting on their knees. Jason and Brandon were helping Linh-Mai in defence because Toby kept gazing dreamily out to sea. The twins, meanwhile, were racing all over the field, playing with the exhilaration Edison imagined they must have felt as young children kicking a ball around on the beaches of their island home.

The Long Island players, finding themselves unchallenged over most of the pitch, gradually moved into Brunswick Valley's end, keeping up a constant attack. Edison dropped back to reinforce the defence, telling Steve as he passed him on the centre line, "If you get the ball, try to keep it while the twins and I get upfield."

Cousin Buddy centred and Edison jumped for the ball, colliding with Junior Green, whose elbow caught him in the stomach. Edison bent double, fearing he was going to throw up. Junior apologized.

Edison said, "It was my fault."

Junior insisted, "It was *my* fault."

The referee handed Amy the ball to restart the game with a goal kick. She sent the ball into the Long Island end and resumed the conversation she'd been having with Cousin Rachel and Toby. "If I lived here I'd spend hours wandering on the beach."

"Not in the winter you wouldn't," said Cousin Rachel. "You'd get blown off it."

"And I'd have a little boat and float around listening to the seabirds calling and the water lapping around the boat …"

"The waves would lap right over you. Remember what it was like on the ferry?"

Toby asked, "Was it rough?"

The Long Island goalkeeper cleared the ball the length of the pitch. It rolled past Toby, who was still talking to Amy and Cousin Rachel. He watched it and a moment later said, "Was that the ball?"

It rolled on to Cousin Buddy, who passed to Junior Green.

Amy was still talking about the island. "The sea is so sparkly and I love the sound of the waves crunching the little rocks …"

Junior Green shot into the net at the same time as he explained, "They used to be big rocks. The reason they're little rocks is they've been pounded so hard by the sea."

A few minutes later Junior hit Toby on the head with the ball when he crossed from the wing. He rushed to him, asking, "Are you all right?"

"Why?" said Toby.

"I kicked the ball and it hit you on the head."

Toby reflected. "Did it?"

At halftime Hannah Guptill looked critically at Shay and Julie, who were sitting on a rock, their heads down, and pronounced, "You two are going to the sick room."

Matthew, who'd left the field halfway through the period, said, "Can I come, too?"

The Long Island coach told Mr. Field, "I'll give you one of my players to keep the sides even."

"No need," said Mr. Field. "The twins do enough running for four."

When the game resumed, Edison thought, *We're a goal down and we look as if we're going to lose the champion-*

ship. And I don't really mind because I'm enjoying the game anyway.

Linh-Mai intercepted a cross from Cousin Buddy and scooped the ball out to Jessica on the wing. Jessica raced into the Long Island end of the field, weaving past one defender and sprinting past another. She centred low across the goalmouth and Edison, struggling to get upfield to support her, reached the ball ahead of a Long Island back. He could try a shot, or he could pass to Jillian, who had stationed herself in the goal area. Without giving himself time to think about what could go wrong with each course of action, he blazed the ball at goal. It flashed just wide of the post.

Steve shouted, "Keep trying!"

A few minutes later, Brunswick Valley broke out of defence again. This time it was Brandon who started the move, sending the ball to Steve, who kept it while Edison ran past. Steve looped the ball high toward the Long Island goal and Edison positioned himself under it. The twins pranced in front of the goal, shrieking, "Here!" Edison set himself to head the ball in their direction, but he didn't meet the ball with the centre of his forehead and it glanced sideways towards the goal. The Long Island keeper, who had run to cover a shot from the twins, could only watch as the ball flew into the net.

He said, "Nice header."

Edison grinned ruefully. "It was a mistake. Sorry."

Steve shouted, "Told you it would pass."

Edison was feeling better all the time, and was already running up the wing when Steve received Jason's pass out of defence and sent the ball on to him. Edison found his way barred by two defenders and passed back, at the same time cutting behind them. Steve staggered a few steps forward with the ball and, as the defenders moved toward him, tapped it between them for Edison to continue upfield. Another defender moved to challenge him. He feinted to go right, and as the defender moved with him, tucked the ball through his legs and collected it behind him, all without breaking stride. Only two defenders remained between Edison and the goal. With no one to pass to, Edison ran full tilt at the first of them, watching the defender's eyes close as he braced himself for the expected collision. Then he swerved around him. As the last defender approached, Edison spun in a full circle, rolling the ball under his foot, so that he passed the defender with his back turned. The goalkeeper crouched ready. Edison looked up, preparing to shoot. He stumbled on a patch of rough grass and crashed heavily to the ground. The Island goalkeeper, watching Edison's fall, took his eye off the ball, which trickled past him into the net.

"Great move," said the keeper.

"Fluky goal," said Edison. "Sorry, again."

A few minutes later, the referee ended the game.

Steve slapped Edison on the back. "Two goals!"

"Two lucky breaks, you mean."

"But now it's passed."

"What's passed?" said Toby, joining them.

"Being a screw-up — and a jerk," said Edison.

11 HIGH PARK

High Park was a huge area of woods and fields in the middle of Dorchester. Mr. Grease steered the van into a line of cars moving slowly on the winding road that led to the school. He parked beside the soccer field, near a cluster of outbuildings behind which the gabled roof of a tall old building rose.

A bell rang and students appeared. They wore blue sweaters and grey pants or skirts. On the far side of the field, spectators were settling along the sideline with lawn chairs, rugs, and picnics. Edison looked for his mother, but he didn't think she'd arrived yet — if she had, she would have been all over him, hugging him and asking him how he was doing and telling him how much she had missed him. He'd been gone for all of three days, after all.

A tall man, with a nose like an eagle's beak and grey hair in a perfect brush cut, marched across to where Mr. Field and the team were clustered by the door of the van. He stood with his feet apart and his hands clasped behind his back and barked, "Good morning, all!"

Mr. Field said, "Hey, man."

The newcomer went on, "I am Morgan Spear, coach of the High Park Memorial Academy soccer team. We're always happy to welcome teams to High Park — and even more happy to beat them."

Edison didn't think he was joking.

Coach Spear swept his arm toward the old building with the gabled roof. "Shall we proceed to the dining hall? Lunch is about to be served. I believe today it's chicken and asparagus casserole, followed by Bavarian apple torte. You'll be our guests, of course."

Toby's eyes widened.

They followed Coach Spear to the old mansion, crossing a lawn like a golf green and skirting a three-tiered fountain on the way. He led them up a steep flight of steps into a wide lobby lined with old team photographs. Edison peered closely at one of them and read beneath the faded black and white picture *Soccer: 1903–4.*

A group of students in red-and-white band uniforms hurried through the lobby with their instruments. They clattered down the steps and headed for the field.

The dining hall was a long room with rows of tables covered in white cloths. Students lining the tables were talking quietly as they ate.

"They have *tablecloths*," said Julie.

"Remember they're to eat off — not to wipe your nose on," said Toby.

★ ★ ★

After lunch they changed in spacious locker rooms with gleaming tile floors and individual showers, then set off for the field. There they found the band parading at one end, while cheerleaders in red-and-white uniforms performed at the other. The crowd of spectators was still growing.

"It's like a carnival," said Toby.

The High Park team was already on the field. They were standing in two lines, their hands behind their backs, while Coach Spear marched up and down in front of them, talking loudly.

Mr. Field led the Brunswick Valley team to the van, where he sat in the doorway. The players sprawled on the grass around him.

Some of Coach Spear's words wafted across the field to Edison. "… One or two good players … some very weak ones, particularly in defence …"

Edison glanced at Linh-Mai and Toby, hoping they couldn't hear.

Mr. Field said, "High Park is the best team in the province, and one of the best in the country. They have scouts, so the players will know our strengths — and our weaknesses."

Toby muttered, "Oh dear."

Mr. Field went on, "So they'll know to mark Steve and Edison closely, and that means we may have to spring a surprise if we're going to score."

"How?" said Steve.

"I'm still thinking. Meanwhile, remember High Park has lots of support, and they mean to intimidate you right from the start. You can bet they'll attack as soon as the whistle goes, and the crowd will roar them on. I'm afraid all you've got cheering for you is Mr. Grease and me, and Mr. Grease isn't too hot in the cheering department."

Mr. Grease grunted.

Toby said, "Do you suppose you could grunt really, really loudly?"

The referee trotted on to the pitch. The cheerleaders formed a pyramid while the band launched into the High Park school song and the spectators roared out the words: *Yes! We are High Park. And yes! We like to win. Play any way you choose. Try any trick or ruse. It really doesn't matter — because you're going to lose! Yes! We are High Park. And yes! We like to win, win, win, WIN!*

By the end of the song, the crowd was in a frenzy, bellowing the last two lines as the band crescendoed with cymbals clashing and drums thundering.

The referee beckoned the teams.

Mr. Field said, "Enjoy the game."

A girl with tawny hair pulled back tightly into a

thick braid that swung behind her like a club shook hands with Shay and said, "I'm Heather, the captain. Sorry you're going to lose."

The referee spun a coin and Heather called, "Heads." The coin fell head-up and she said, "We'll take the kickoff." She added, with a dazzling smile, "And we'll score right away."

Amy was chattering beside Edison. "This is the *most important* game I've ever played in. Well, I haven't really played in that many games but this is most *definitely* the *biggest*. There must be more people here than in the *whole* of Brunswick Valley. I wonder if I know anyone in the crowd. My mother has a cousin who lives in Dorchester and she's got kids so …"

From Amy's other side, Toby advised, "Concentrate on the game. Remember Mr. Field said that High Park will attack right off."

"Right," said Amy. "I'm concentrating now, Toby. Don't worry." A few seconds later she started, "I love how our blue uniforms look against High Park's red and white …"

On the sideline, Mr. Field was greeting Mrs. Flood. She waved to Edison and he waved back discreetly.

In the centre of the field, he and Steve faced Heather and her fellow striker. Heather was a head taller than Edison, and wider in the shoulders. While they waited for the whistle to start, she said, "This is Harry." She jerked her head at her teammate. Harry dwarfed Heather in both height and width. He had close-set eyes and a crooked nose. His black hair gleamed like a wet bathing cap. His eyes were fixed on Amy's goal and he didn't seem aware that Heather was introducing him.

Heather went on, "We're going to give you a whipping. We know about you two." She smiled at Steve. "You're Steve and you'll get mad if we crowd you and you're no good when you're mad — right?" She turned her smile on Edison. "And you're Edison-Superstar-Who's-Lost-His-Nerve." She stopped smiling and added, "Don't expect to find it here."

12 NO FUN

When the referee whistled for the kickoff, the band burst into the High Park school song, while the cheerleaders rattled tambourines and the spectators roared even louder than before.

Edison had to admire the accuracy of Heather's prediction, as well as how efficiently High Park scored right from the start. At the whistle, Heather back-heeled the ball to one of her midfielders, who kept it while the strikers barrelled up the field. The midfielder lofted the ball into Amy's penalty area, where Harry, rising easily above Linh-Mai and Julie, nodded the ball across the goalmouth to Heather, who calmly slotted it past Amy.

Looking back from near the centre line, Edison thought, *We all kept our positions perfectly, and we did everything right, but we're a goal down. If we'd hustled, we might have stopped them.*

The noise from the crowd and the cheerleaders and the band rose until Edison thought it couldn't get any higher.

But it could — when High Park scored again.

This time it was Heather who rifled the ball into the net from Harry's pass, after he had charged through Matthew's half-hearted tackle and rounded Toby easily on his way to sending her the ball.

The half was nearly over before Brunswick Valley mounted its first attack. Steve and Edison had been carefully marked by the home defence, with one marker always at their heels or standing right in front of them, and another close by.

It was easy to see their plan for Steve. They were simply going to harass him all the time, frustrating his usual wide-ranging movement around the pitch. One defender was always practically standing on his cleats, and Edison saw Steve lash out angrily when the defender held his shirt as he tried to start a run.

Edison was getting the intimidation treatment. His marker had clattered into him the first time he went for the ball, knocking him over. Two days ago, this kind of treatment would have upset him so much that he would have avoided the ball as much as possible. If he got possession, he would have passed the ball before the marker had time to make him look stupid and weak. Now he knew how to handle it. The next time he got the ball and the marker crowded him, he turned and faced him. The marker lunged at Edison, his foot scything at the ball. Edison skipped backward, easily avoiding the tackle, and waited for him to try again. The marker lunged, and Edison repeated the maneuver. He sensed the other marker approaching from behind, and when the front marker lunged again, Edison skipped sideways so the marker coming from behind crashed into his teammate, while Edison dribbled the ball away.

Julie ended another High Park attack by scrambling the ball out of the Brunswick Valley goal area to Matthew. Edison slipped away from his marker to make himself available if Matthew wanted to pass. He glimpsed Steve doing the same. Two more defenders were moving in on Matthew, who hesitated, seeing the way ahead barred. He made a half-hearted feint to the left. The defender read the move easily and took the ball from him. Instead of trying to regain possession, Matthew threw up his arms in a gesture of hopelessness.

A few minutes later, Jillian took the ball down the wing. Edison moved wide of the goal, taking his two markers with him and opening up space for Jessica, who was moving in from the other wing. The goalkeeper moved out to cover Jessica. *Now*, Edison thought, *Jillian can do the safe thing and centre the ball, but the goalkeeper will probably outjump Jessica — so no goal. Or Jillian can try to dribble around her marker and rush at goal, giving herself an outside chance of scoring while the goalkeeper is distracted by Jessica.* The second move was risky, because if Jillian lost possession, High Park would launch a quick counter-attack. But she needed to take the risk. Brunswick Valley badly needed a goal.

Edison watched as Jillian played it safe, centering the ball.

As the goalkeeper caught it, Edison realized his teammates were playing like they had in the first two games of the tour. They were so conscious of looking like a winning team that they forgot their success had come from playing with such fun and enthusiasm that they scrambled for every ball and never stopped hustling their opponents.

He thought, *We're certainly not enjoying ourselves now.* They were two goals down, the first half was drawing to a close, the crowd was against them, and the championship was disappearing fast.

13 SURPRISE

At halftime, while the band marched up and down the field, the cheerleaders performed somersaults and pyramids, and the crowd kept up a constant cheer, the Brunswick Valley students stood and sat around their van.

Mrs. Flood, who'd been hovering near the bench, beckoned Edison. "Mr. Field says it took you a game or two to adjust to Brunswick Valley's style of play, but now you're getting better all the time."

He grinned. "It's a lot different from playing at Canterbury."

"It looks as if your team is going to win easily."

He started, "But we're two goals down …" Then he realized she was talking as if he was already playing for High Park. He said, "Brunswick Valley's my team."

"Of course, dear, but … Well, you know what I mean. Do you think I should speak to Coach Spear now?"

"I think you'd better wait until after the game."

"You're playing very well, but Brunswick Valley isn't. I hope that won't affect Coach Spear's assessment of you."

As Edison rejoined the team, Shay grumbled, "We're playing like kindergarten kids."

Mr. Field corrected him. "You're playing like a team more concerned with looking like champions than with enjoying the game."

Edison burst out, "You're playing like I was! You're afraid of not looking good."

"You know who we should play like, don't you, Edison?" said Mr. Field.

Edison smiled and said, "The Dorchester All Stars."

"Right," said Mr. Field. "Their expectation is to enjoy the game! Winning comes second. You've got to have the same expectation. And to prepare for it, have a scrimmage over there." He pointed to a meadow of rough grass at the end of the pitch.

Toby grabbed a soccer ball from the van and kicked it in the direction Mr. Field was pointing. Everyone chased after it. Edison reached it first, with Linh-Mai close behind. As he tapped it to Steve, he tripped and fell. Linh-Mai tripped over him, and Julie fell over her. Steve had the ball and kept it just out of reach of the twins, daring them to tackle him. Amy sneaked up behind and reached her foot around his ankles to steal the ball, but Edison, scrambling to his feet, raced between Steve and the twins, taking the ball with him.

He stopped and turned. Julie and Linh-Mai were advancing on him. Toby was lumbering after everyone, holding a rock in each hand. He called, "The boys' goal is between this rock ..." He threw one down. "... And this one." He placed the second rock about a metre from the first and stood between them, adding, "I'm the goalkeeper."

"That's not a goal," said Linh-Mai. "It's a ... a ... mousehole."

"So where's the girls' goal?" Julie demanded.

"There." Toby pointed at two young hawthorn trees growing nearby. They were about ten metres apart.

As Toby pointed, Edison chipped the ball over Linh-Mai and Julie. Toby kicked it into the girls' goal and performed a little dance, proclaiming, "Boys — one. Girls — nil."

Edison looked across the meadow to where the High Park players were lined up before Coach Spear. Their attention seemed to be more on the Brunswick Valley pickup game than on their coach.

When the referee walked onto the pitch for the start of the second half, Mr. Field gathered his players quickly to him. "We have to find a way of springing a surprise on High Park if we're going to score, because most of the time they've got you guys ..." he nodded at Steve and Edison "... bottled up."

Edison nodded, and Steve said, "Tell us about it."

"Their close marking is part of my plan," said Mr.

Field. "This is what we're going to do." The team leaned closer as he lowered his voice to describe the surprise move.

When he finished, Shay said, "That's crazy."

"That's why it'll be a surprise," said Mr. Field. "But remember — we can only pull this stunt once. We have to hope it unsettles High Park enough for Steve and Edison to do their stuff."

"I have an idea for a surprise too," said Edison. The team collected around him as he described his plan. It was a move the Eagles used to do. He finished uncertainly, "Do you think it'll work?"

"It'll be fun finding out," said Mr. Field. "Now — forget about winning or losing, and forget about expectations and reputations. Play with as much fun as you played in the meadow."

When the game resumed, High Park swept straight into the attack. Heather passed to Harry, sending him on a run at the Brunswick Valley defence. He left Brandon standing, brushed past Toby, and cantered toward Amy's goal with only Linh-Mai left to beat. She planted herself in Harry's path, her eyes fixed on the ball. He slammed into her. She staggered backward, but managed to keep her feet and gave chase. She caught up and was about to tackle when one of his pistoning elbows cracked her on the forehead. She reeled backwards and collapsed. The referee whistled and waved Mr. Field and Mr. Grease on to the field.

"I'm *okay*," Linh-Mai protested, struggling to her feet. "Stop making a fuss."

As Mr. Field returned to the sideline, he whispered to Shay and Edison, "First chance you get — spring surprise number-one."

A few minutes later, when Edison took the ball past Heather, she launched into a sliding tackle from behind. As her foot stabbed the ball from his feet, he made sure he tripped over her leg and fell. The referee whistled.

Heather protested, "I got the ball."

The referee said, "Free kick." He pointed to a spot halfway between the midfield and the Brunswick Valley goal. Edison placed the ball and backed up, ready to take a long run for the kick.

Coach Spear shouted, "Stay close to your assigned player."

Edison started his run at a slow trot. He gathered speed as he went down the field, and was in full flight by the time he swung his leg to kick the ball. At the last second he slowed. Instead of kicking the ball, he passed his foot over it, then back-heeled it. At the same time his teammates burst into a frenzy of action. The twins set off running in a wide circle, following one another. Their markers moved with them, so that the four players ran in a circle. Shay and Steve raced toward their own goal. Their markers looked at Coach Spear, who called, "Stay with them!" Matthew and Brandon were on opposite sides of the field. They ran toward each other, passing in the middle. When they reached the opposite wing, they turned around and set off across the field again, their markers on their heels. Toby, Linh-Mai, and Julie, who had waited near the Brunswick Valley goal while Edison prepared for the kick, raced toward the High Park goal, overtaking Edison, who veered toward the wing. His marker tracked him closely. The ball, meanwhile, had rolled a few centimetres and stopped. As Edison headed for the wing, all his teammates, taking their cue from him, did the same. Their markers followed them, leaving the centre of the field empty — except for one player.

Amy had sprung from her goal as soon as Edison headed for the wing and was racing down the pitch. She collected the ball without stopping and careened toward the High Park goal.

Coach Spear screamed, "Never mind who you're supposed to be marking. Stop her!"

Amy, with only the High Park goalkeeper to beat, veered left. The keeper went with her. Amy swerved right, rounded the keeper, and stroked the ball gently into the net.

Apart from a polite smattering of applause, the crowd and the band and the cheerleaders were silent.

The only voice was Mr. Field's. "Sur-prise!"

As the game resumed, the High Park band struck up again and, with the cheerleaders' encouragement, the crowd roared its support for the hometeam.

Mr. Field tried to make himself heard above the noise, shouting, "We need two more goals. Two more!" He repeated, clapping with the rhythm of the words: "Two more! Two more!" Mr. Grease clapped too.

When they stopped, the chanting and clapping continued. "Two more! Two more!"

Edison heard the chant change from the coach's hoarse voice to a lighter, higher sound, and looked across the field. Another minibus had pulled up behind Mr. Grease's, and Casey was leading the Dorchester All Stars in the chant. As Edison watched, she pushed through the crowd with her companions, and they lined up behind the Brunswick Valley bench, still chanting and clapping. Ella waved to him. He waved back, then turned his attention to the game.

Jillian had received the ball from Jessica's throw-in and had sent it into the High Park penalty area. A defender cleared it, but only as far as Matthew, who dribbled past his marker and chipped the ball back into the centre. It landed at Edison's feet. Two defenders immediately challenged him. With no space to move, and no one unmarked to pass to, he kicked the ball against one of the defenders. It rebounded out of play for a throw-in near the Brunswick Valley bench. Mr. Field retrieved the ball. As he tossed it to Edison he murmured, "I think it's time for another surprise." Edison nodded and waved Brandon over to take the throw. Brandon threw the ball to Edison, who set off toward the High Park goal, his two markers at his heels. He gathered speed, then stopped abruptly, so that both of them crashed into him.

The referee whistled and said, "Free kick." He placed the ball where Edison had fallen, about sixty metres from the High Park goal.

Edison called, "I'll take it."

At the same time Steve shouted, "I'll take it."

They both ran to take the kick. Edison got there first and stood over the ball. Steve pushed in front of him. The High Park players were looking at one another, grinning.

Shay ran across. "I'm captain and I say Steve takes it."

Edison complained loudly, "It's my turn to take a free kick."

By now their opponents and the spectators were laughing so much some of them were doubled over. Heather called, "Do you always carry on like this in Hicksville?" Edison caught a glimpse of his mother with her hands on each side of her mouth. She was glancing uneasily at Coach Spear.

The referee said, "Make up your minds."

Shay said, "We're ready. Steve's taking it."

Steve pushed Edison aside and backed up in preparation for taking the kick. As he started his long run up, Edison also started running, picking up speed until he crossed Steve's path. Then he slowed. Coach Spear called urgently, "Watch them! They're up to something," but his warning was almost inaudible against the laughter of his team and the crowd.

Steve flicked the ball sideways. Edison took two steps with it before stroking it with his foot so that it soared toward the High Park goal. At first it looked as if it would fly over and wide of the goal, but at the last second it bent and dipped and rocketed under the crossbar into the top corner of the net.

Mr. Field's shout of "One more!" was picked up by the Dorchester All Stars. Mrs. Flood was smiling and applauding. She had moved closer to Coach Spear.

As the half wore on, with Brunswick Valley pressing for a winning goal, High Park retreated into a defensive wall, and Edison began to fear the game would end in a tie — a fair result, but not one that would earn Brunswick Valley the championship. He caught Mr. Field's eye and pointed to his wrist to ask, *How much longer?* Mr. Field held up one finger.

Edison watched as Shay intercepted a loose ball near Amy's goal and slotted it into Steve's path in the centre of the field. Steve raced to it and, without looking up, punted it ahead and chased after it. Heather barred his way and Harry was barrelling in from the side. Edison had stationed himself near the halfway line. He slipped away from his marker, so that he was free for a pass, knowing Steve would be aware of him. Steve, his head still down, crashed into Heather at the same time that Harry charged him from the side. Steve stabbed the ball toward Edison as he fell.

Edison set off toward the High Park goal, thinking of what Mr. Field had said — *just play ... enjoy yourself* — and the carefree spirit with which the Dorchester All Stars played. He could hear their voices chanting above the noise of the crowd. As he listened, he forgot all the special coaching he had received at the elite camps, and the drills he had been put through by all the advanced-level coaches he'd been sent to. He forgot that he was supposed to be a soccer prodigy, a star in the making. Instead, he thought only of how much he loved to dribble and kick and run with a soccer ball.

He eluded the tackle of the first defender by pushing the ball right as he went left, rounding the defender before collecting the ball on the other side. He passed his next challenger by feinting left, then stepping over the ball and pushing it right as he changed direction and followed it. From the corner of his eye he glimpsed his mother. She was talking to Coach Spear, who was nodding his head as she pointed to Edison. Harry, racing back, nearly intercepted the ball, but Edison put his foot on it and rolled it out of the path of the striker's swinging foot before cutting behind him, as his momentum carried him past. Now only two defenders were between Edison and the goal, facing him side by side. He heard Heather's feet thundering from behind. He kept going until he was almost in the faces of the pair of defenders, then turned abruptly and faced Heather. He tapped the ball between her feet and jumped sideways. As she crashed into the defenders, Edison retrieved the ball and turned toward the goal. He gave the ball a final push ahead and chipped it over the head of the advancing High Park goalkeeper — into the net.

★ ★ ★

When the game ended, Coach Spear approached Edison as he left the field. He shook Edison's hand and said, "Congratulations on winning the game for your team. High Park was the better side — I'm sure you'd agree with me if you weren't surrounded by your friends — but you made the difference. Brunswick Valley owes the championship to you."

As Mrs. Flood hugged Edison, she whispered, "Coach Spear is *very* impressed. He says you're in!"

14 NERVE

Edison and his friends waved as the Dorchester All Stars left High Park Academy. With hands and arms waving from every window, their mini-van looked like a strange multi-limbed insect. Casey had promised to bring her team down in the spring for an exhibition game with Brunswick Valley School.

Mr. Field said, "We'd better get on the road too. Your parents are expecting you home tonight."

Edison looked around for his mother. She expected him to travel with her, but he didn't want to go straight home. Toby and Linh-Mai and Steve were going for pizza in the little Brunswick Valley Mall before they went home, and had asked him to join them. They wanted to tell him about the soccer games they played when the regular season ended. Linh-Mai had already described some of them — the five-a-side street league in the dead-end road she lived on, the indoor games at the Boys and Girls Club through the winter, and the scrimmages every Saturday morning with some kids from Pleasant Harbour, Brunswick Valley's neighbouring town. Sometimes, she'd told him, they even played in the cemetery, although they weren't supposed to. Toby said if they got caught, there would be, "grave consequences."

Mrs. Flood, smiling broadly, was hurrying from the school buildings with Coach Spear. She waved and called, "Coach Spear wants to talk to you."

Edison looked at Mr. Field.

He said, "Go on."

Coach Spear was holding a file. He opened it, leafed through some papers, and said, "We have a dossier on you. It's very impressive." With a glance at the faces of Edison's friends peering from the van, he led Edison and Mrs. Flood further away, speaking quietly and earnestly. "We'd like to offer you a soccer scholarship to High Park Academy, starting as soon as you complete the transfer from Brunswick Valley." He shook hands with Edison again. "We look forward to seeing you on the High Park team, which, on the evidence of your play here today, will surely lead to a place on both the provincial junior team and the national youth training squad. Congratulations!"

He nodded to Edison, shook hands with Mrs. Flood, and marched away.

Edison's mother hugged him. "I'll see Mr. Justason tomorrow and tell him you're transferring to High Park. Then we'll go shopping in Saint John and get your uniform and some new clothes. You'll find that the students at High Park dress quite ... er ... differently from your friends at Brunswick Valley. And we'll call your father tonight. He'll be so proud. Then ..."

Edison blurted out, "I don't want to go to High Park."

He couldn't believe he had said it. When had he decided? Was it during the game? Or after it? His Brunswick Valley friends had surrounded him, the girls hugging him, the boys pummelling him, and Linh-Mai saying, "You were really great," as she looked at him, then looked down quickly.

Mrs. Flood was looking at Edison as if he'd passed wind loudly. "But it's what we planned for you — ever since you left Canterbury."

"Sorry."

She frowned. "You're just nervous about the move. You'll get over it."

"I won't change my mind."

"You'll feel differently in the morning. We'll talk about it then."

He felt torn in two. He wanted to please his mother, and he knew how proud she and his father would be if he played for High Park and attended school there. He could imagine his mother telling her friends at work about him. She would probably mention him on TV, in the bit at the end of the news when she chatted with the weather man. He was afraid she would be more than disappointed. She'd be hurt.

But he didn't want to go to High Park any more. He still wanted to play soccer — serious soccer — at a high level, but he wanted to do it while playing for Brunswick Valley.

"You're overtired," Mrs. Flood went on. "There's too much to think about, isn't there?" She hugged him again and said, "Go on. That adorable van's waiting for you."

"Don't you want me to come with you?"

"Of course I do — but you'd rather be with your friends, wouldn't you?"

He grinned and nodded. He took a step toward the van. Mr. Field was standing by the door and Mr. Grease was already at the wheel. His teammates were watching.

He looked at his mother. Her eyes were shiny. "Thanks, Mom."

"Call me when you're ready to come home. Then we'll talk some more."

"Mom, I *really* don't want to go to High Park."

She patted his cheek gently. "We'll see."

When Edison climbed in the van, Steve burst out, "What did Coach Spear want?"

Edison took his usual seat between Steve and Linh-Mai. Shay and Julie hung over the back of the seat in front, while his teammates in the seats behind stood and leaned forward.

"He wants me to play for High Park. He offered me a soccer scholarship."

Mr. Field whistled. "That's worth several thousand dollars."

"Think of all the famous players who started their careers at High Park," said Shay.

"What else did he say?" Linh-Mai asked.

"He said I'd get in the provincial junior team and the national youth training squad."

"You'd be one step away from playing for Canada," said Julie.

"You'd be famous," said Shay.

"We'd see you on TV," said Toby.

Steve smiled ruefully. "I was looking forward to you and me getting lots of goals together." He reached across Linh-Mai and shook Edison's hand. "Congratulations, buddy. I'll miss you."

Linh-Mai said, "It was nice having you playing with us, even if it was for just a few games."

"What do you mean?" said Edison.

"Well if you're playing for High Park, you won't be playing for Brunswick Valley."

"Who said anything about playing for High Park?"

"You did — just now."

"Coach Spear did," Edison corrected her. "I didn't."

Linh-Mai smiled slowly. "Don't tell me you turned him down."

"I'm going to."

"Your mother will go spare," said Toby.

Edison nodded.

Steve grinned. "You've got nerve."

Other books you'll enjoy in the
Sports Stories series

Basketball

❑ *Fast Break* by Michael Coldwell

Moving from Toronto to small-town Nova Scotia was rough, but when Jeff makes the school basketball team he thinks things are looking up.

❑ *Camp All-Star* by Michael Coldwell

In this insider's view of a basketball camp, Jeff Lang encounters some unexpected challenges.

❑ *Nothing but Net* by Michael Coldwell

The Cape Breton Grizzly Bears prepare for an out-of-town basketball tournament they're sure to lose.

❑ *Slam Dunk* by Steven Barwin and Gabriel David Tick

In this sequel to *Roller Hockey Blues*, Mason Ashbury's basketball team adjusts to the arrival of some new players: girls.

❑ *Courage on the Line* by Cynthia Bates

After Amelie changes schools, she must confront difficult former teammates in an extramural match.

❑ *Free Throw* by Jacqueline Guest

Matthew Eagletail must adjust to a new school, a new team and a new father along with five pesky sisters.

❑ *Triple Threat* by Jacqueline Guest

Matthew's cyber-pal Free Throw comes to visit, and together they face a bully on the court.

❑ *Queen of the Court* by Michele Martin Bossley

What happens when the school's fashion queen winds up on the basketball court?

❏ *Shooting Star* by Cynthia Bates

Quyen is dealing with a troublesome teammate on her new basketball team, as well as trouble at home. Her parents seem haunted by something that happened in Vietnam.

❏ *Home Court Advantage* by Sandra Diersch

Debbie had given up hope of being adopted, until the Lowells came along. Things were looking up, until Debbie is accused of stealing from the team.

❏ *Rebound* by Adrienne Mercer

C.J.'s dream in life is to play on the national basketball team. But one day she wakes up in pain and can barely move her joints, much less be a star player.

❏ *Out of Bounds* by Sylvia Gunnery

Jay must switch schools after a house fire. He must either give up the basketball season or play alongside his rival at his new school.

❏ *Personal Best* by Sylvia Gunnery

Jay is struggling with his running skills at basketball camp but luckily for Jay, a new teammate and friend has figured out how to bring out the best in people.

Ice Hockey

❏ *Deflection!* by Bill Swan

Jake and his two best friends play road hockey together and are members of the same league team. But some personal rivalries and interference from Jake's three all-too-supportive grandfathers start to create tension among the players.

❏ *Misconduct* by Beverly Scudamore

Matthew has always been a popular student and hockey player. But after an altercation with a tough kid named Dillon at hockey camp, Matt finds himself number one on the bully's hit list.

❏ *Roughing* by Lorna Schultz Nicholson

Josh is off to an elite hockey camp for the summer, where his roommate, Peter, is skilled enough to give Kevin, the star junior player, some serious competition, creating trouble on and off the ice.

❏ *Home Ice* by Beatrice Vandervelde

Leigh Aberdeen is determined to win the hockey championship with a new, all girls team, the Chinooks.

❏ *Against the Boards* by Lorna Schultz Nicholson

Peter has made it onto an AAA Bantam team and is now playing hockey in Edmonton. But this shy boy from the Northwest Territories is having a hard time adjusting to his new life.

❏ *Delaying the Game* by Lorna Schultz Nicholson

When Shane comes along, Kaleigh finds herself unsure whether she can balance hockey, her friendships, and this new dating-life.

❏ *Two on One* by C.A. Forsyth

When Jeff's hockey team gets a new coach, his sister Melody starts to get more attention as the team's shining talent.

❏ *Icebreaker* by Steven Barwin

Gregg Stokes can tell you exactly when his life took a turn for the worse. It was the day his new stepsister, Amy, joined the starting line-up of his hockey team.

❏ *Too Many Men* by Lorna Schultz Nicholson

Sam has just moved with his family to Ottawa. He's quickly made first goalie on the Kanata Kings, but he feels insecure about his place on the team and at school.

Soccer

❏ *Lizzie's Soccer Showdown* by John Danakas

When Lizzie asks why the boys and girls can't play together, she finds herself the new captain of the soccer team.

❏ *Alecia's Challenge* by Sandra Diersch

Thirteen-year-old Alecia has to cope with a new school, a new step-father, and friends who have suddenly discovered the opposite sex.

❏ *Shut-Out!* by Camilla Reghelini Rivers

David wants to play soccer more than anything, but will the new coach let him?

❏ *Offside!* by Sandra Diersch

Alecia has to confront a new girl who drives her teammates crazy.

❏ *Heads Up!* by Dawn Hunter and Karen Hunter

Do the Warriors really need a new, hot-shot player who skips practice?

❏ *Off the Wall* by Camilla Reghelini Rivers

Lizzie loves indoor soccer, and she's thrilled when her little sister gets into the sport. But when their teams are pitted against each other, Lizzie can only warn her sister to watch out.

❏ *Trapped!* by Michele Martin Bossley

There's a thief on Jane's soccer team, and everyone thinks it's her best friend, Ashley. Jane must find the true culprit to save both Ashley and the team's morale.

❏ *Soccer Star!* by Jacqueline Guest

Samantha longs to show up Carly, the school's reigning soccer star, but her new interest in theatre is taking up a lot of her time. Can she really do it all?

❏ *Miss Little's Losers* by Robert Rayner

The Brunswick Valley School soccer team haven't won a game all season long. When their coach resigns, the only person who will coach them is Miss Little ... their former kindergarten teacher!

❏ *Corner Kick* by Bill Swan

A fierce rivalry erupts between Michael Strike, captain of both the school soccer and chess teams, and Zahir, a talented newcomer from the Middle East.

❏ *Just for Kicks* by Robert Rayner

When their parents begin taking their games too seriously, it's up to the soccer-mad gang from Brunswick Valley School to reclaim the spirit of their sport.

❏ *Play On* by Sandra Diersch

Alecia's soccer team is preparing for the championship game but their game is suffering as the players get distracted by other interests. Can they renew their commitment to their sport in order to make it to the finals?

❏ *Suspended* by Robert Rayner

The Brunswick Valley soccer form their own unofficial team after falling foul to the Principal's Code of Conduct. But will they be allowed to play in the championship game before they get discovered?

❏ *Foul Play* by Beverly Scudamore

Remy and Alison play on rival soccer teams. When Remy finds out Alison has a special plan to beat Remy's team in the tournament, she becomes convinced that Alison will sabotage her team's players.